Circle of Prey

Marlene Mitchell

BEARHEAD PUBLISHING
- BhP -
Louisville, Kentucky

Circle of Prey

BEARHEAD PUBLISHING
- BhP -
Louisville, Kentucky
www.bearheadpublishing.com/marlene.html

Circle of Prey
by Marlene Mitchell

Cover Design by Bearhead Publishing
Cover Concept by Marlene Mitchell

First Printing - February 2009

ISBN: 978-0-9799153-8-3
1 2 3 4 5 6 7 8 9

Disclaimer

This book is a work of fiction. The characters, names, places, and incidents are used fictitiously and are a product of the author's imagination. Any resemblance of actual persons, living or dead, is entirely coincidental.

.Proudly printed in the United States of America.

Dedication

To my sisters, Betty and Virginia,
my brother, Donald, and his wife Melba.
I love you all.

Other Novels by Marlene Mitchell

Yard Sale - Everything Must Go

Return to Ternberry

The Chester County Boys

The Women of Magnolia

The Beginning of the Circle

Houston Ferrell called his son, Garrett into his office. He was irritated at the latest report he had received about Garrett's behavior. It was twenty minutes before Garrett answered the call and sauntered into the office.

"I understand that one of the employees working for you has committed suicide. Her name was Jeannie Owen. Did you know her?" Houston asked.

"Vaguely. Why is this any concern of mine?"

"I'm tired of all your antics, Garrett. I know damn well that you were seeing her. What did you do this time? I cannot afford another one of your scandals. If it's not a woman, it's drugs or gambling debts. You're a married man, you have a son, and it's time to step up to the plate."

Garrett leaned back in the chair. "And what exactly does that mean?"

"It means it's time for you to stop acting like a spoiled brat and take on more responsibility in this office," Houston replied angrily.

"Does that mean I am being promoted to vice-president?'

Houston rubbed his hand across his forehead. "You are so far from that position I am not even going to answer that question. I want to make you corporate head of the finance division. You will be working closely with the other men on this floor. If you do a good job, we'll talk about a promotion in a couple of years."

"Bullshit! Keep your job. I'm your son. Doesn't that count for something?"

"I thought it did, but you have proved me wrong. Here is my final offer. Take the position or I will give you and your family an equitable allowance to live on and you can leave this office and go wherever the hell you want. Go to Africa and kill another elephant. That should make you happy. I want your answer by Friday."

Garrett stood up and leaned over the desk. "Is that a threat?"

"You can take it however you want, but this time I am serious. Dead serious."

On Thursday morning, Houston arose from his bed and padded down the winding staircase to the kitchen. He opened the refrigerator and took out a carafe of orange juice. Pouring himself a small glass he moved to the counter and plugged in the coffee maker.

The explosion was so forceful that it ripped through the ceiling and out of the roof on the second floor. Flames immediately engulfed the kitchen.

The firefighters arrived four minutes later, but were unable to save the house. Cynthia Ferrell was called at the Florida resort where she was vacationing and informed of her husband's death. Garrett was awakened at his apartment and also given the news.

Two weeks after the funeral the investigation into the cause of the devastation listed it as an electrical overload, which sparked and caused the gas explosion. Although the evidence was sketchy, there was no reason to expect foul play. The alarm system was still in place and all of the gates and doors to the house were secured.

Within weeks Garrett Ferrell had been named president of the company. Cynthia decided to go to Monaco and continue her grief at the gambling casinos.

Birth

In a fourth floor walk-up apartment in Brooklyn, New York, Rosa Charpelli squeezed her husband Frank's hand as pain tore into her stomach. The mid-wife stood at the foot of the bed, towel in hand, waiting to catch the baby as it struggled its way out of Rosa. Quietly enduring the agony, Rosa raised her head from the pillow and pushed with every ounce of strength left in her. Minutes after the birth, she cuddled her new son. He would be called Michael Dominic Charpelli. She held him close to her while her husband looked on with pride.

At a private hospital in West Hampton, New York, Marguerite Ferrell screamed in pain as the doctor and three nurses tried to calm her. After just a few hours of labor, Marguerite insisted that the doctor take the baby by cesarean. When he refused, a phone call was made to her husband, who was at his office in New York City. Within fifteen minutes she was wheeled into the delivery room. Her son would be called Elliott Bryant Ferrell. He was taken from his mother and carried to the nursery so that Marguerite could rest. She would look in on him later.

Bayanni stood under the canopy of acacia trees hiding from the dangers of the open plain. In the distance the rest of the elephant herd waited. After her twenty-two month pregnancy, they paced nervously while the matriarch of the herd gave birth to her calf.

Bayanni's almost inaudible guttural sounds alerted the herd that her time was near. Standing close to her was her sister, Yamaya. She would help Bayanni if there were difficulty in the birth. Bending her legs, Bayanni struggled to stand as a gush of water escaped from her body. With one last heaving thrust, the calf slid from beneath her legs and landed on the ground. He lay there quietly for a few minutes and then raised his head. Sneezing and snorting he tried to clear his lungs. The mother and her sister tenderly stroked his head and supported his neck with their trunks. Within thirty minutes he was standing and flapping his ears. He was perfect except for an odd birthmark. On his left ear there was a perfect white circle the size of a saucer dish where the skin pigment was devoid. In a few hours, Bayanni and her young son were able to rejoin the herd and begin their long journey to a new feeding ground. He would be called Jakuta.

Chapter One

Frank Charpelli stepped off the gangplank of the Franca C. Steamship and into a mass of people crowding the dock. He stopped for just a second and made the sign of the cross. He could not believe that he was in New York City. He had finally made it to America. Someone bumped into him and muttered the word, "move!" Frank stepped to the side, answering the crowd, "scusi, scusi." Clutching his packet of papers to his chest he followed the signs to the port authority office. He took his place in line behind the dozen or so other men and women. When it was his turn, he proudly stepped up to the counter and handed the clerk his papers. A broad grin covered his face.

"You speak English?" the man behind the counter asked. Frank continued to smile at him. "Parl een-glazay?" the man asked.

Frank made a gesture with his two fingers, "Si, muiy capito."

The man opened the papers. "Do you have relatives here? Relativos?"

Frank shook his head no.

Another question, "Do you have a sponsora?"

Again the answer was no.

"You have a request for entry from the governor of Salerno so you have one week to find a place to live, appartamento, and find a job, a posizione…capisci, you capisci?"

Frank nodded. The man stamped the papers. "You be back here in one week with proof and we will talk about extending your visa."

"Next," the man called out, waving Frank away.

Along with his papers, Frank carried a paper bag that contained a shirt and a pair of underwear. He had sixty-seven dollars in his pocket. Frank wore only a light jacket. The weather in Mola di Bari had been warm when he left Italy. Now, his face and hands were numb from a cold he had never felt before as he hurried along the dock.

Walking the busy streets of New York City, it took Frank only a few hours to find a job at an Italian bistro. They liked the idea that he could speak Italian. It added to the ambiance of the restaurant. Cleaning off tables and doing dishes seemed so easy compared to working on the fishing boats in his hometown.

The same day he rented a room in a rundown boarding house. Frank didn't care about the sagging bed or soiled carpet. Comfort was not one of his goals. His father's words were his driving force. "You go to America. You get an education and make lots of money. You make us proud." He had heard those three sentences since he was a child. And now he was here…in America to make his family proud and hopefully make a lot of money some day. With a new job and a place to live Frank's visa was granted.

A week later Frank stood in front of the television set in the restaurant and cried with the other patrons and employees when the news that John Kennedy had been assassinated filled the screen. He made the sign of the cross. He must remember that even in America bad things happen to good people.

When Frank got his first paycheck, he found a thrift store just a few blocks from his rooming house. For six dollars he came out of the store with an armful of clothes and two bath towels. He stopped at the post office and mailed an envelope containing two dollars to his parents.

Frank was now ready for his second step of his journey. He had to find out where the adult education classes were being held. One of the other busboys at the restaurant helped Frank find the school and fill out the necessary paperwork to register in night school.

At PS26, Frank enrolled in an English class that he would have to attend three nights a week. He was excited. He wanted to learn the language of his new country and quickly!

On the first night of class, Frank arrived early. He had walked the eleven blocks to the school, not sure enough of himself to attempt riding the bus. He carried a notebook and pencil that he had bought at the drugstore and slipped into a seat in the back row. In the chair next to him was a young woman with her hands folded on the desk. Maybe it was her dark hair and eyes that made him think she was also Italian or maybe it was just the softness in her face that made him smile at her. She smiled and nodded to him. Her name was Rosa Deleon. She was from a small town just inland from Mola Di Bari and like Frank, she spoke just a few words in English.

Frank began to look forward to seeing Rosa in class. He had someone to talk to in his native language and it helped to ease the pain of loneliness he felt. He missed his parents and siblings and at times wanted to go home. Rosa too was lonely. Her parents were upset that she had not decided to become a Sister of Mercy like her older sisters. Rosa had always pictured herself married and having children, something her parents did not see happening. Rosa had been sent to America to take care of an elderly aunt who had never succumbed to the American way of life. Rosa felt that she was being punished. Her aunt had lived in America for most of her life yet she had never learned the language well enough to communicate with others. Rosa needed to learn English so that she could interpret for her aunt who had become bedridden. Her aunt did not trust anyone, so Rosa was to take care of all of her affairs and the house.

It was on the night of his third class that Frank noticed Rosa walked with a limp and the fingers on her left hand were twisted and small. He had only seen her at her desk, but today they arrived at class at the same time. She seemed embarrassed as he walked beside her. He did not ask questions. He would let her tell him in her own time.

That night after class Frank invited her to join him for coffee. They sat across from each other in the small restaurant around the corner from the school.

Rosa smoothed her dress and folded her hands on the table. "I have only a few minutes," she said in Italian. "My aunt will be very upset if I arrive home late. You have not asked me about my affliction?" she said.

"It is none of my business," Frank replied.

"I had polio when I was a child. I was one of the lucky ones. Over fifty children in my town died. But now I have a useless hand and a bad limp."

"That doesn't change who you are," Frank said, smiling.

Rosa smiled back at him. He had made her feel at ease.

As their conversation continued, Frank told her about his parents that still lived in poverty in a small two-room cottage in Italy. He promised them that he would make a lot of money and help to make their life better. He was proud of the fact that he was already able to send them a few dollars each week since both of his parents were in ill health.

How long does it take before you realize you love someone? A week, a month…six months. Frank and Rosa knew they had feelings for each other in less time than that, but anything other than a friendship was out of the question. She had her responsibilities with her aunt and he had to work and go to school. Yet, after a few months while Rosa's aunt slept, Rosa would quietly open the door for Frank. They would sit in the parlor and talk quietly. Sometimes he would hold her hand and if she permitted, he would kiss her. She could not believe that someone was really interested in her. He felt the same way.

Frank took quickly to the English language and started his high school classes with all the excitement of a child on Christmas morning. Rosa did not fair as well. She had difficulty with spelling and math. After she learned enough English to translate for her aunt she decided to stop going to class. They were both sad that they could no longer see each other as often, but Frank knew that Rosa was struggling with the studies and it was causing her much distress. It made the time they spent together even more precious. Each time they were together their resistance for each other was becoming weaker. They were very much in love. They decided to limit their visits to keep from letting the devil tempt them further.

Frank's math teacher was impressed with his ability to do difficult problems while the rest of the class lagged behind. He encouraged Frank to find a job where he could use his skills every day. After searching the classifieds every day for two weeks, an ad appeared that peaked his interest. Frank applied for the position and after two interviews he became an employee of the shipping division of Ferrell Enterprises.

Working on the loading docks, he was in charge of making sure that the cargo unloaded into the warehouses was the same as the bill of laden that came with it. With his pad and pencil in hand, he counted the pallets as they were taken from the ships and logged their contents into the records making sure that none was damaged. He was good at his job.

It took him only two years to complete the high school courses before he was rewarded with a diploma. Although he longed to be with Rosa he knew that getting his education was his first priority. They saw each other whenever he had a few hours to spare. She knew he was very tired. Working long hours through the day, he enrolled in the city college for night classes. Frank wanted to major in accounting. He would be Frank Charpelli, Certified Public Accountant. Frank also decided it was time to study for the citizenship test. He was worried that if something happened to Rosa's aunt, she would be sent back to Italy. He needed to become a citizen so that he could marry her.

When Frank was in his first year of college, Rosa's aunt died. Rosa fell into his arms and cried, "What am I to do now? I don't want to leave you. I know they will take my visa from me and send me back to Italy since I no longer have any reason to stay here."

"You will marry me, Rosa, and as my wife you can stay here with me. We love each other and we should be together."

Teary eyed, she smothered his face with kisses. "With what I get from my aunt we should do fine. We will have a home and you can quit your job and focus on your education. It will be good for both of us, Frank."

Several days after the funeral, Frank and Rosa sat in the attorney's office. The attorney opened the sealed document and began to read. Rosa's aunt left everything she owned to her church. That included her house, all the furniture and the money in her bank account. She left Rosa her rosary and prayer books.

Rosa stood up and screamed. "I spit on her grave. I cared for that mean, old woman for almost five years and she leaves me nothing, not even the bed I slept in. I spit on her grave!"

Frank had never seen her like this. Her face distorted in anger, she screamed her words of vengeance. "Rosa, please, calm down. Don't be greedy. She brought you to America and gave you a good home. Be thankful for that."

"Greedy! You call me greedy, Frank! I cleaned her house, cooked her food, and washed her body and none to her satisfaction. She treated me like a slave. I had so little free time to spend with you and never any money to buy myself even a new handkerchief and you call me greedy for asking for just a little in return." Rosa covered her eyes and burst into tears. "She promised me that she would take care of me when she passed. She lied."

Frank wished he could take back what he had said. He tried to comfort her. "I will take care of you. Please, Rosa don't cry. I promise I will give you the life you deserve."

The attorney, feeling uncomfortable at this point, folded up the will. "You have a right to contest this will Miss Deleon, but when it involves the church it is usually very hard to win." He excused himself and left the room.

With her young son walking close to her, Bayanni guided the herd along the dusty trail to a new destination. It was the herd's duty to keep the newborns out of harms way. With wary eyes they watched the plains for signs of predators, ready at any minute to defend their young. The innocent would follow the lead of the elders. They would gather strength and learn new experiences every day.

Chapter Two

Frank and Rosa were married at the Sister's of Mercy Convent where Rosa went every day to pray since moving to New York. The nuns were closely connected with their sister convent in Italy. It gave her comfort to go there and pray in Italian.

Frank and Rosa moved into a fourth floor walk-up in the Brooklyn Borough. There were two small bedrooms, a living room and a kitchen you could hardly turn around in. Within a few weeks, Rosa had scrubbed every inch of the apartment with a brush and lye soap. It was quite a bit less desirable than the house she lived in with her aunt, but she was with Frank and it was her home. It was all they could afford if Frank was going to continue going to school. Rosa took a job in a neighborhood laundry where she cleaned the clothes of others, while her own laundry sat in a basket in the apartment. Frank hated the idea that she had to work, but the extra dollars helped to make their lives a little better. With the extra money, they bought the foods they loved and Frank surprised his wife with a small television set on their first month anniversary. It gave Rosa something to do while he was away every night at school.

At times Frank felt guilty that he had to spend so much time studying and in class. He wanted to spend more time with his wife, but whenever he brought it up, she would smile and hug him and tell him she understood. He also felt guilty that he could not do more for her. So for the next three years they shared their love and made do with whatever came their way. It was a simple life, but it was filled with laughter and true feelings for each other.

Three weeks before graduation Rosa broke the news to Frank that she was pregnant. He was overjoyed. A baby! It would complete their family. He had no idea how he would support his growing family, but he was too happy to worry about it.

He never knew that Rosa harbored a secret. She was told after her bout with polio that having a child was almost out of the question for her. Her twisted bones would make a delivery almost impossible. She prayed each day to the Virgin Mary that she could someday conceive and give Frank a child.

"I hope we have a daughter, Frank," Rosa said as she sat in her chair by the window. It would be better to have a girl since you and I are so short. Short girls don't take the teasing that small boys do."

"Nonsense, Rosa. Look at me. I never let it bother me. Let them make their silly jokes. It only shows their ignorance. You don't have to be tall to be rich and we will be rich someday."

When the baby was born, Rosa wanted to give him an Italian name. Frank disagreed. "No! Our son is an America citizen. He needs a strong name, a good American name." After some deliberation, he was named Michael Dominic Charpelli. Frank conceded on his middle name since it was the same as his father's.

With a wife and a new son, Frank knew it was time to start moving up the ladder of success to provide a better life for them. With his diploma hanging on the faded wallpaper in the living room he made an oath to Rosa that the next year he would be making more money.

Each Monday, Frank would arrive early at his job. He would log onto the company's employment page and read the job openings. And each week, Frank would submit his application to whatever position was open. It was a process he would continue for the next two years. He never wavered and never gave up the idea that someday he would move up the ladder in the Ferrell company. After graduation he had been promoted to accounting manager in the dock office but that was not good enough for him. His desire was to work in the downtown office. He wanted to wear a suit to work everyday and carry a briefcase. It would make him feel important, but, for now, nothing could surpass the pride he felt in his new son and his wonderful wife.

After another six months a notice was posted that an entry-level accountant was needed in the downtown corporate office. Frank was excited. The pay was just a few dollars more than he was making, but…it was in the corporate office. Pulling the paper off the board, Frank folded it in half and headed for his own small office. Within hours he had a crisp copy of his resume on the way to the personnel division.

Bayanni guided the herd down the last steep grade before she finally let them rest. Trumpeting and guttural sounds for the last twenty miles let her know that they were exhausted and wanted to stop. She knew better. They had been without water much too long. Another day would mean losing more of the herd. Stepping off the slope she sank into the cool mud, the water bubbling up around her feet. She nudged Jakuta forward and he instinctively began to prod the ground with his trunk. Within a few minutes all of the elephants were in the channel of muddy water. Bayanni was no longer anxious. She had done her job. She had provided for those that depended on her and now they would be safe for a while. Tomorrow they would move into the vast plain of swaying golden grass and eat from the fruit and leaves of the acacia trees. The feathery palms and huge water-bloated Baobab trees would greet their old friends. They would gain back the weight they had lost during the trip and be content with their new environment for a while.

Chapter Three

"Oh, Frank, do you think we can afford it?" Rosa asked. Her footsteps echoed across the floor of the empty house. "It is so nice. I love the kitchen and such a nice backyard for Michael. That will be wonderful."

Frank laughed. "Yes, we can afford it. It isn't a palace you know."

Rosa threw her arms around her husband's neck. After living in the cramped apartment for six years this house was a castle to her. With three bedrooms and a proper bathroom where you could actually turn around without hitting your head, it would be wonderful.

It was just a small craftsman bungalow on a tree-lined street in Flushing Meadows. Yet to Rosa it seemed like a palace. There were sidewalks and neighbors and a clothesline in the backyard. No more carrying groceries up four flights of stairs with a two-year-old lagging behind. Michael could have friends and maybe she could, too. Rosa knew she would love living in this house. Frank could imagine himself playing ball in the yard with his son. Life would be good in the new house.

Each night when Frank returned home from work his attention turned to his family. After eating dinner it was his time with his son. Watching Michael dash around the house, climbing on everything and laughing gave Frank a sense of pride. In the summer after Rosa finished the dishes, the three of them would go for a walk. It was a favorite time for all of them. They stopped to talk to neighbors and exchanged smiles and greetings with anyone who passed by them.

In the evening, Frank would bathe his son and read him a story while he lay in bed protesting the idea of going to sleep. Frank would kiss his head and tell him he loved him. Michael would throw his arms around his father's neck. The love was returned as he grew older each year.

Michael loved winter in New York, especially at Christmas time when he was off from school. He loved waking up to fresh, white flakes that had fallen during the night. Glistening in the sunlight the snow beckoned to him. His mother always obliged. Dressed in three layers of clothing and rubber boots he would run through the yard creating his own artwork in the snow.

When the Christmas lights were put up in the city, Michael would join his mother and father in the traditional trip to the downtown streets of New York. He marveled at the decorated windows and listened to his father as he explained that someday when they were rich he could go into any of the stores and buy anything he wanted. That is what money can do for you, Frank would tell his son. Later, Frank would drive his family through the wealthy areas of town emblazoned with colored lights and Christmas displays. And then again he would remind Michael that when they were rich they would live in one of these neighborhoods and have the best display of all. It really never mattered to Michael. He was happy and so was his mother. They had everything they needed in their lives. It was only his father that was driven by the need for affluence.

When Rosa reminded Frank that she didn't think it was a good idea for him to put these kinds of ideas into a child's head, Frank would answer with, "He won't be a child forever, Rosa. He needs to prepare himself for this future. Good grades and diligence will get him into a good college."

Rosa would roll her eyes. "For heaven sakes, Frank, he is only six years old." Frank would laugh and once at home they would eat supper in the kitchen with their elbows on the table and talk about what Santa was going to leave under the tree.

In one of those large estate houses, which had an outside Christmas display that lit up all three stories, another six-year-old boy was eating his dinner. He had a white linen napkin draped across his lap and took sips of water from his crystal glass. He ate in silence. His parents had left for the evening, leaving him at home with his nanny. A twelve-foot tree ablaze with lights stood in the living room. The tree surrounded by brightly wrapped gifts. A reminder to the boy that it was not Santa Claus, but his father that gave him presents.

It was early spring and the Savannah was in the throes of mating games by all of the plains animals. The mature bull elephants had moved closer to Bayanni's herd searching out the females who were in estrus. As a large bull approached her, Bayanni raised her trunk and bellowed, giving him the signal for them to pass on by her. She was nearing fifty years of age and too old to produce another calf. In her adult lifespan she had given birth to fourteen calves, with six of them surviving to adulthood. Her maternal time was over. The bull puffed a few times and turned away.

Chapter Four

When the doctor finally told Rosa that she should give up trying to have more children she was devastated. She had suffered three miscarriages after the birth of Michael. "I wanted lots of babies," she cried. "I wanted two boys and two girls and now I am told there will be no more." Her hands covered her eyes as she sobbed.

Frank tenderly put his arm around her shoulder. "I know you are sad, Rosa, but we have Michael and for that we should be grateful."

"I understand that, Frank, but he is growing up so fast. He doesn't seem like a child anymore. He is so self-sufficient. He locks me out of the bathroom and insists that I knock when I come into his room."

"He is just trying to assert his independence. We have smothered him since he was born. He loves you, Rosa. I am sure of that."

Independence was not the only trait that Michael was exhibiting. He had become a fearsome opponent against his father at chess and handball. At school, he excelled in all of his studies, plus soccer and swimming. Seeing the pride on his father's face when he competed made him happy. He was a winner. Losing was something he did not accept very easily.

Michael's wall was decorated with ribbons and medals he had won in school competitions. There was a wall of pictures taken by his father as he was presented with his awards and trophies.

"You push yourself too hard," Rosa told her ten-year-old son. You should have more fun and not worry about winning all the time."

"I like to win. Besides Dad says that a winner will always be noticed and rewarded for their hard work. Someday I am going to be rich."

Rosa shook her head. She didn't like hearing that from her son. She had told Frank over and over that he should not make everything he and Michael did a competition. It was beginning to grate on her nerves. Even the daily routine of the house was turned into an arena. Running to see who could get the mail first, who could finish their drink the fastest, and who would be in charge of the remote control for the evening. The words, "I win, you lose," was heard often in the house.

In a private, all boys' school in Westchester another young man was proving his ability to win. Playing polo, chess and cricket he was a formidable match for all the other male students. His parents were never there to see him compete.

Frank continued to climb the corporate ladder at Ferrell. Each year he was rewarded with a promotion and moved up another floor. His diligence was paying off. When Michael was twelve his father received a huge advancement. Moving to the eighteenth floor of the Ferrell Corporate Offices, the nineteenth floor was now within his reach…just one step away to the top of the ladder. Along with the promotion, Frank was given a large raise, more than doubling his salary.

"We need to move, Rosa," Frank said. The Sunday classifieds lay open in front of him. "There are some very nice houses on Long Island that I would like to look at. Also, I have decided instead of sending Michael to a parochial school we'll enroll him in a private school. I understand that Mr. Ferrell has a son just about the same age as Michael. I'll try to find out tomorrow where he attends."

Rosa almost dropped the dish she was washing. "Move! Oh no, Frank, I don't want to move. I love this house and this neighborhood. Surely you're not serious. All of my friends are here and Michael loves his school."

"Oh, but I am serious, Rosa. We can afford a much better home than this one. We can have a pool and a garage for the new car I am going to buy. Michael can have a recreation room in the basement where he can invite friends from school. It will be very good for all of us. We can even join a country club. Michael can make new friends. It will be good for him."

No amount of protesting from Rosa could convince Frank that they should not move. He was convinced that he was doing the right thing for his family. Michael was apprehensive about the move. He had always been the best at everything he did at his present school. How would he fare some place where he knew no one?

After months of looking, Frank and Rosa bought a house on Long Island. Rosa knew that no matter how many houses she looked at she would never be happy away from her house in Flushing. The new house was much too large and expensive. It was a two-story, white brick with a three-car garage. A covered patio complete with a cabana and in-ground pool took up most of the back yard. Like all the other houses in the sterile environment it had a manicured lawn and large trees that alienated them from their neighbors.

Michael was enrolled in the Westchester Academy for young men. Dressed in his new tan pants, white shirt and blue blazer his father drove him to school on the first day. When the car came to a stop in front of the school, Frank turned to his son, "Are you afraid of going to a new school, Michael?"

"Dad, I'm twelve years old. Why would I be scared? I'm not a baby anymore. I can take care of myself."

Frank Charpelli smiled at his son and opened the car door. Michael took a deep breath and made his way up the stairs. He was scared to death.

The first morning of school went smoothly with a few stares at the new kid from the other students. At lunchtime Michael carried his tray across the noisy cafeteria looking for an open seat. Spying a space at the end of a table he maneuvered through the crowd. He set his tray down and started to sit down.

"Hey, you can't sit there," he heard someone say.

"Why not?" he asked.

"Because I said so, just go on find another table." Before he could pick up his tray the boy who made the remark pushed it across the table sending it crashing to the floor. All of the boys at the table, except for one, began to laugh. Without thinking Michael grabbed the boy by the front of his shirt and lifted him off his seat.

"You pick it up right now or I'm going to kick your ass," Michael said, his face just inches from the boy's face. The room seemed suddenly quiet as the boys at the table quickly moved away. The boy began to whimper. Michael let go of the boy's shirt. "Go on, get the hell out of here." He reached down on the floor and picked up the unopened sandwich and his milk. He finally composed himself enough to notice that one boy was still sitting at the table calmly munching on an Oreo.

Michael swung his feet over the bench and sat down. He was shaking. His stomach was churning. He had no idea where he got the strength to stand up to his challenger. His father's voice echoed in his ears. *Don't be a bully, Michael, but don't let anyone push you around. You have to stand your ground.*

"What's your name?" the boy said.

"Michael Charpelli."

"You're pretty brave or pretty stupid. I'm not sure what. It's not a good idea to make enemies on the first day of school." He grinned. "You sure scared the crap out of Justin. I'm Elliott Ferrell. Those kids are my buds. They do what I say and they know I don't like anyone sitting at my table unless I say it is okay. You're cool so I'll let you sit here." Another twelve-year old boy was bragging.

"My dad works for a man named Garrett Ferrell, is he any relation?" Michael asked.

"Yeah, he's my dad. I guess we got a problem. I'm not allowed to associate with any of my dad's employees. Too bad. I kind of like you. Come on, I'll show you around anyway, Meatball," Elliott said, grinning.

Somehow being called Meatball didn't seem so bad to Michael when it came from his new friend. Walking the halls of the school, they were not to be tampered with. Elliott, tall and blonde and Michael, short with black hair made an odd pair, but they were becoming the best of friends. Elliott liked this kid he called meatball who would stand up to him and Michael like the foul-mouth kid named Elliott who would take any challenge given to him. They became formidable adversaries for all those who challenged them. They found that the most fun was to test each other and as time passed their stunts became more and more daring. It was a one-upmanship that would continue for years. It was all about getting even and seeing who could come up with the next adventure to test each other.

It was Elliott's idea to keep their friendship secret from their parents. Elliott said his father was adamant that Elliott not fraternize with any of the children of his employees. This time Elliott was not going to listen to him. He liked Michael and as long as he only used his first name his father would never know or care who his new friend was.

Elliott spent more time at the Charpelli home and when Frank Charpelli asked him what his father did for a living, Elliott answered, "He works in the stock market."

Elliott was amazed at the amount of interaction that Michael had with his parents. He was not used to family meals or parents sitting together in the same room watching television. At times it was enjoyable for him to be a part of something and at other times he was envious of Michael.

Michael was introduced to Elliott's parents as Michael Davis, a friend from school who had come to spend the week-end. They were really not interested in Elliott's little friend and breezed on past the two boys as they left for an evening out.

It wasn't until Michael and Elliott were in college that they didn't see any reason to keep their friendship a secret. Frank was particularly pleased, but Garrett frowned and said he would have to get to know Michael better before he could give his approval to a friendship that was already almost ten years old.

Jakuta had left his mother's side and joined the young bulls on the perimeter of the herd. He was almost as tall as her, yet his juvenile ways still showed as he tousled with the other young males. They would push and shove each other in an effort to win the games that would prepare them for later life. It was only when the large, mature bulls came around that they would scatter and go back to the safety of the herd. They were far from strong enough to venture out on their own, much less challenge a bull twice their size. Occasionally Bayanni would pass close by her son. They would recognize each other. He would lower his head and make an inaudible sound, which she clearly understood. He would remember her all of his life.

Chapter Five

The wind whipped through the long corridor leading to the quadrangle. Michael held his blazer close to his body and lowered his head. Just as he turned the corner he was met head on by someone crashing into him. Falling to the ground, Michael reached for his glasses that lay on the sidewalk. He could not see without them.

"Oh man, I'm so sorry, Mike." The voice came from the blurred vision next to him. Michael put on his glasses.

"That's okay, Elliott no harm done, I think," Michael said, brushing off his pants and standing up.

"Are you sure you are okay? It was my fault. I was in a hurry. I'm freezing my ass off. Should have brought a coat to school today. Sorry I didn't see you."

"No problem, I'm fine," Michael replied.

"At least let me buy you a cup of coffee," Elliott said. "I'm on my way to the cafeteria right now."

"You're on," replied Michael. "I've been up almost all night cramming. I could use a cup of coffee."

The two boys said little as they moved across the open lawn. It was too cold to talk.

They settled at a table in the middle of the cafeteria after getting coffee. "So how was your Christmas holiday? Did you go anywhere?" Michael asked.

"I went skiing in Aspen. My parents were supposed to go, but as usual they never showed up. My dad is too busy to even say hello to me and my mother decided to stay in town and do the social circle. My old man is a pain in the ass. It's all about the business and social status. And my mother, well, she is so full of herself. She's had so much work done on her face her eyebrows are almost on her forehead," Elliott said, laughing. "What did you do over the holiday?"

"Nothing much. Just spent time with my parents. Ate too much and slept a lot."

"Sounds good to me. I hate spending time with my parents. All they do is argue."

Michael smiled, but he wasn't really amused. He had never heard anyone speak so disrespectful of his parents. Michael's parents meant the world to him and he loved them both. He never found it funny when Elliott talked about his parents.

"So, I suppose when we graduate you are not going to work at your father's company?" Michael asked, wanting to change the subject.

"You better believe I am. He has offices all over the world. I'll just pick one far enough away from him so we don't cross paths too often. Of course, right now we're getting ready for our annual hunting trip. I've asked you to come along every year, Mike. Come on and go with us this time. It will be a lot more fun for me with you along."

"You know how I feel about killing animals, Elliott. We've had this conversation many times. I wouldn't think killing an elephant could bring anyone enjoyment. I think they're pretty amazing animals."

"Hell, it's great. There you are out in the bush, just you and your rifle against an animal ten times more powerful than you. You wait until he is in your sight, until you are looking straight at each other, then you hesitate and give him a chance to retreat. They seldom do. Then you slowly pull the trigger and watch as they fight to stay upright. It's the ultimate challenge between man and prey. There are those first few seconds that you know if you don't shoot, he will surely charge at you. It's a real rush." Elliott seemed mesmerized as he talked. "We're going to the eastern part of Africa in late summer, after the rainy season. My father is bound and determined to bag an elephant on this trip. He came home without one for the last two years. It sure puts him in a foul mood."

Elliott looked at his watch. "I have to run or I'll be late for class again." He picked up his napkin, wadded it up and pitched it toward the trashcan. It fell to the floor. As he walked over to pick it up, Michael tossed his and it landed in the container. "Two out of three," Elliott said, as he picked up another napkin and crumpled it up.

"You're on." Elliott threw the last napkin from the holder into the trashcan. "Now, we're even," he said.

Michael stayed in the cafeteria for a few minutes after Elliott left. He ran his fingers around the coffee cup remembering the time a small yellow kitten that his father brought him home was killed by a car. He loved that kitten and the day she was killed he stood by the window and watched his father shovel her remains out of the street. They buried her in the backyard. How could anyone kill an elephant?

Life was good on the Savannah. The rainy season had passed and the tall grasses provided shelter and food for many of the plains animals. Bayanni watched over her herd, which had increased with six new calves born in the past month. Like all the other females, she took her turn tending to the young ones to keep them safe. It was an abundant time, with plenty of food and water to drink and bathe in. Yes, life was good...for now.

Soon the mood of the herd would change. The dry season would once again be upon them and it would be time to start their migration to the other side of the Savannah. Some of the young bulls were now ready to leave the herd. They had spent the time of plenty testing their strength against each other and some had been singled out to be driven from the herd and lead their solitary life. Jakuta was long overdue to be on his own. On his last day as part of the herd he raised his trunk and let out a thunderous bellow and then trotted away from the others. Bayanni turned and watched her son leave. She was nearing seventy years of age, yet she was able to bellow back at him. He stopped for a moment and then walked away.

Chapter Six

The two men, both in black suits, sat in the leather chairs facing the desk of Garrett Ferrell. They were silent, waiting for Garrett to speak first.

Garrett tapped his pencil on the paper in front of him. "So tell me, what do you know about Frank Charpelli?"

The first man cleared his throat. "Mr. Charpelli is an immigrant from Italy. He has a college education and has been working for you for over twenty years. He is meticulous in his work. He follows orders and has hopes of someday working on this floor. He is driven by money and talks about money, frequently.

"Family?" Garrett asked.

"Wife and one son. They live on Long Island. Frank knows how to manage a dollar and does quite well for himself. His son is in college," the man added.

"What about relatives?"

The other man answered. "None in this country. His parents passed away years ago. He has one older brother still living in Italy, but he is not in good health."

"Tell me about his wife?" Garrett asked.

"She's a housewife. Her name is Rosa. She has very little education. She still has a few friends in her old neighborhood, but no living relatives in this country. She is partially paralyzed and doesn't get around very well. Mrs. Charpelli does not drive or go out much."

"Thank you, gentlemen," Garrett said. They both stood up and like wooden soldiers turned and marched from his office. Garrett pushed his intercom button, "Carol, tell Mr. Woodson to set up a meeting for tomorrow morning with Frank Charpelli." Garrett swiveled his chair around and surveyed the view from his nineteenth floor office. He smiled to himself. Garrett has found his man.

The invitation to join the other eight men who had offices on the nineteenth floor came as a complete surprise to Frank. He read it over several times, looking around to see if perhaps someone was lurking about ready to tell him it was all a prank.

Frank had only been at his position on the floor below for a little over four years, not long enough to earn this kind of advancement. He was honored that Garrett Ferrell thought his qualifications were strong enough to move to the top floor and become part of the elite group running the company.

On the day of the meeting, Frank awoke early and took extra precaution shaving, hoping his five o'clock shadow would not show up early. He trimmed his sideburns, brushed his teeth twice and put on his most expensive suit. When he kissed Rosa goodbye that morning Frank had no idea how his life and the lives of his family were going to change.

The morning elevator ride to the nineteenth floor seemed to take forever. When the car finally stopped and the doors opened Frank stepped out onto the plush green carpet that ran the length of the hallway. There were huge plants along the wall and soft music playing. He felt as if he were in a five-star hotel. Stopping at the receptionist's desk, Frank smiled and gave her his name. Within minutes another woman escorted him to the conference room.

Even though Frank was early, Garrett was already present. He sat in the large chair at the head of the long table.

"Frank, it is good to see you," Garrett said, reaching over to shake his hand.

Frank had only met Garrett Ferrell on a few occasions. He was surprised at the friendly greeting. It was common knowledge that Garrett Ferrell liked to keep his employees at arm's length, except those in his inner circle. His policy was to hire competent people to run his business on the lower floors and allow him to make the major decisions in regard to the men on the nineteenth floor.

Garrett cleared his throat. "I'll be honest with you, Frank, I have been watching you for some time now. I feel that your credentials are just what I am looking for to fill in a very critical position in this company. I suppose you were informed in the company bulletin that Ralph Jillion had a fatal heart attack last month. We are all deeply saddened, but it is important for me to replace him as soon as possible. He was a critical part of my team and you, Frank Charpelli, qualify for his position."

Frank was stunned. He could hardly speak. "Thank you," he said in an almost inaudible voice. "Are you sure?" he asked.

Garrett seemed annoyed. It was not the response he expected. "Why, Frank. Is there some reason why you feel you're not qualified for this position?"

"No!" Frank said, too loudly. "It's just that this is something I have dreamed about for years. I just wanted to make sure that I am hearing correctly."

Garrett feigned a smile. "You heard correctly." He stood up. "And now I would like to introduce you to the rest of my team."

The door opened and Frank watched as a parade of men, all dressed in dark business suits came into the room and took seats around the table. Garrett was also watching them as they entered. "*Look at them. They're all a bunch of sniveling idiots. If they only knew that what they do in this company is only a pittance compared to what I do. Someday I won't need them, but right now they are a necessary evil to keep everyone on an even keel.*"

"Gentlemen, may I introduce to you, Mr. Frank Charpelli, the new Division Head of the Morritt division." Someone began to clap and the others followed suit. Frank slowly rose from his chair. "Thank you, thank you, all. I hope I can do as good a job for you as Ralph Jillion." A hush fell over the room.

Drinks and trays of food were brought to the boardroom as everyone began to congregate around Frank. By the end of the afternoon he knew all the names and positions of the other eight men. Sometime during the festivities Garrett left the room. That would be Frank's last cordial encounter with his new co-workers.

When Frank arrived home that evening he tried to tell Rosa what had happened but he seemed to babble from too much scotch and the heady feeling from what was one of the best days of his life. He awoke the next morning still not quite able to digest it all.

Frank's new office was the last in a row of mahogany doors that lined the inner offices. His assistant's name was Carol Grey. She had been working on the nineteenth floor for many years and knew what was expected of her. Within two days she had the office exactly as Frank wanted it. Even though the massive and very expensive furniture remained, Frank had the sports memorabilia that Ralph Jillion loved removed. He replaced it with pictures of wife and son and a large map of the world. He waited patiently for someone to tell him what he was supposed to do.

Carol began to fill him in on the details of the operation. She was so knowledgeable about everything that Frank was surprised they had not given her the position.

"I noticed that you have referred to me as your secretary several times, Mr. Charpelli. Actually, I am not a secretary, but more of a go-between for the companies you will be doing business with. Now, I would like to give you a few guidelines that will help you get started. The computer screen in front of you will be your most important link to your clients and also to the other officers on this floor. Mr. Ferrell is annoyed with the constant ring of telephones. He feels that the employees on the floors below us should take care of most of the communication that comes over the telephone."

Frank interrupted her. "Really? I always felt that talking to someone personally is an important business tool. This all seems so impersonal."

"Mr. Ferrell likes to keep it that way. He wants all of our contacts to be on a strictly business level," Carol said. "Each of the employees on this floor are available to you by entering their name or code into the computer. Overseas clients are also dealt with in this manner also. It helps us to keep accurate records of everything that transpires. Telephone contact is permitted only with permission from Mr. Ferrell."

Frank laughed. "Honestly, you're not serious. It sounds like Hal…you know the computer in that space odyssey film."

Carol frowned, "Please! Mr. Charpelli, do not ever refer to our system as Hal in front of Mr. Ferrell. He has spent millions of dollars to develop a sophisticated system designed especially for our company." She seemed quite annoyed with Frank.

"I'm sorry, Carol. May I call you Carol?"

"Yes, that would be fine, Mr. Charpelli. Now let's get back to work."

Frank was now in control of the finances of several overseas importing and exporting divisions. It would be his job to make sure that all the money funneled in and out of the companies was carefully monitored. He would be in charge of all the accounting of merchandise that was sent through international waters. A huge job at best, but Frank was ready for the challenge. He would have to depend on Carol to help him.

Carol returned to her office and opened the personal file on Frank Charpelli. He had an impressive record with Ferrell. She wondered what was the real reason that Garrett selected him for such a prestige position in the company. He certainly did not have the credentials that usually impressed Garrett. Carol hoped that maybe, just maybe, Frank was an honest man and that he would not be put into the mix of underhanded activities that every person who held that job before him was sucked into. She would try to make sure that it didn't happen again.

Each day seemed to bring a new set of rules. Some were easy to follow and others more difficult. Frank was given a memo from Mr. Ferrell that stated Frank should disassociate himself from the subordinates in the offices on the lower floors. Mr. Ferrell believed it was not in Frank's best interest since he was now in a position of power. The memo disturbed Frank. He had made many friends over the years. How could he tell them that he could no longer be their friend? Did he even want to do that? Rosa, too, would be upset. She had become friendly with some of the wives. Garrett had made sure that all of the other employees in the company that Frank associated with on a personal basis were told that it would no longer be possible for him to do so and they were not to contact Frank or say anything about the memo they received. It was a direct order from Mr. Ferrell himself. They all knew that it was an order you did not ignore.

The position came with an astronomical salary that Frank was ill prepared for. He could not believe what he was now making. The first constructive suggestion he was given was from Ari Goldman. Ari was the corporate head of the legal division for all the Ferrell Enterprises' employees. His office was directly across from Frank's. Ari told Frank to set up an overseas account and deposit some of his earnings in it to protect him from a huge tax burden. "Trust me, Frank," Ari said convincingly. "When you start making six figures you have got to do something to protect yourself. Even Mr. Ferrell has several overseas tax shelters that he puts money into."

Frank said he would think about it.

Jakuta trotted across the open plains toward the herd of females. Several of the cows had been giving off the scent of estrus. They would wait for him. He was in charge.

He circled around the herd several times before picking his mating partner.

Chapter Seven

"Hey, Meatball! What's this I hear about your father?" Elliott said as he neared the table where Michael was sitting.

"What did you hear?" Michael asked.

"I heard he moved into the big time…on top of the mountain now."

"He's happy. He has what he always wanted, which is more money than he can spend. My pop is a really good guy and if that makes him happy, that's okay with me."

"So money doesn't mean that much to you, Meatball?" Elliott asked.

"I never said that. Someday I want to be richer than him."

"Want to bet on that?" Elliott laughed. "You know I get the whole thing when my father dies. I'll have billions before you make your first million."

"Who knows, maybe he'll live to be a hundred and give me time to catch up." Michael replied.

"By the way," Elliott said, "The hunting safari is scheduled for late August. You interested in tagging along?"

"Africa…sounds interesting, but I'm not really into hunting. I could come with a camera. What would your father think about me tagging along? I thought this was some kind of bonding time for the two of you?

"Bullcrap! I've had enough bonding to last me a lifetime. Every time we have one of those sessions it usually involves something I have done wrong. Go with me. It will keep him out of my face. As long as he gets his elephant he'll be happy."

When Michael called his father and told him that he was going to Africa with Garrett and Elliott Ferrell, his father was elated. Anything Michael could find out about Garrett Ferrell would be helpful to him. Since Frank had been at his new position Garrett once again had become an elusive figure that he rarely saw. Once a month he would stop into the board meetings for a few minutes and disappear just as quickly. Frank was proud of the work he was doing for the company, but the figures on the sheets that were reviewed each month were the only thing that seemed to matter. Perhaps Michael could break through that hardcore exterior that surrounded Garrett Ferrell.

Michael had certainly gotten past all the barriers that seemed to stand in the way of him and Elliott becoming friends. He ignored Elliott's jokes about his height and the fact that Elliott preferred calling him Meatball most of the time. They had found a common ground in their competitive nature and played it to the hilt. They pitted themselves against each other on a daily basis—whether it was a poker game or tennis or a game of chicken with ski mobiles. Sometimes they wagered money, other times it was just a matter of whether either of them was crazy enough to do what the other asked.

Over the past two years they had gone deep into an underground cave, skydiving and bungee jumping off cliffs in Acapulco. The rush they got when they knew that they had done something uncommon and lived to tell about it replaced their fear. It was always on a dare by one or the other...neither willing to back down. Most of the time it was not about winning, but getting even, making sure they were just as good as one another. Frank and Rosa were concerned about Michael's adventures with Elliott. To keep from causing them more anxiety, Michael stopped telling them what he and Elliott were doing.

Michael and Elliott disagreed on how parents were to be treated. Michael loved his parents dearly and would do almost anything for them, while Elliott felt nothing but disdain for his and only wanted his father's money. Michael cringed when Elliott referred to his mother as the bitch.

They also disagreed on women. Michael liked safe relationships with coeds who he respected. Elliott would laugh at Michael's choices. He would usually show up at a frat party with a girl from a local strip bar or some rich heiress draped on his arm. He prided himself on being a ladies man, even though none of his relationships seem to last more than a week or two.

Several bulls had moved into his territory. Jakuta charged into the herd with all the ferocity he could muster. Flapping his ears and snorting dust from his nostrils he engaged in battle with the first male elephant he encountered.. Soon blood was running down Jakuta's side from the sharp tusk of the other male, but he stood his ground and charged again. After a few minutes the tussle was over and Jakuta was once again the victor and able to mate with the cow.

Chapter Eight

When the corporate jet landed in Mozambique, Michael had no idea what time it was. He sat up in bed. He had a splitting headache from staying up almost the entire trip and playing cards with Elliott. Between them they had finished off two fifths of Chavez Regal costing over three hundred dollars a bottle. Even twenty-five year old scotch gave him a headache and he had no idea if he had won or lost or came out even.

"Dammit! I got a bitch of a headache. My eyeballs feel like they are going to drop out," Elliott said holding his head as he sat up. "How about you?" he asked.

"Don't talk to me. I think I am going to throw up." Michael ran for the bathroom. When Michael emerged from the bathroom, Garrett was standing in the aisle, fully dressed. He had gone to his private quarters as soon as the plane had taken off.

"If you two gentlemen are done with your foolishness I suggest you get dressed. Let's have no more of this until after the hunt." He turned and departed from the airplane.

"Well I guess I didn't make a very good impression on your dad," Michael said, wiping his mouth on his sleeve.

"Piss on him. He is so damn perfect he makes me sick. I'm here to have a good time. Let's get dressed and go kill an elephant and then we can party some more." Elliott stood up and groaned.

Their luggage was loaded into the Land Rover for the four-hour trip to the EMO Safari Club. Both Michael and Elliott cringed each time the driver hit a bump or swerved to miss a water buffalo standing in the road, hoping that they could make it all the way without getting sick. After they arrived at the plush compound and were shown to their rooms it was dinner-time before either of them surfaced.

Garrett stood in the lounge holding a drink in his hand. "You're late. They're holding dinner for us. They ate in silence. When the waiter took away the last plate, Garrett stood up. "I expect your behavior to improve as of right now," Garrett said in a stern voice. "We are here on a serious mission, not to get drunk and play stupid games. Are we clear?"

Michael smiled. "I'm sorry, Mr. Ferrell, but I can't really believe that you are this intense about elephant hunting. I thought you called it a sport?"

Elliott nudged Michael under the table, a signal to him to stop talking. He could see his father's jaw tightening.

"We'll see, Mr. Charpelli. We'll see who has the last laugh tomorrow. Now if you'll excuse me I'm going to retire for the night. I suggest you two do the same."

Early the next morning, dressed in a new bush outfit, Michael left the club with Elliott, Garrett and two Malawi guides in the Land Rover. He was handed a sleek, high-powered rifle, which he promptly laid on the seat and picked up his field glasses. He watched the landscape change and realized he was now the intruder in this primordial land. Michael would catch glimpses of shadowy figures moving about in the bush.

The roads were rutted and dusty and insects buzzed around his face even though he had lathered himself with repellent. Stopping at intervals, large herds of grazing animals would pass in the distance. Thousands of animals, zebras, gnus, Cape buffalo and giraffes moved in unison like a choreographed dance. Each one seemed aware of their destination and unconcerned with the presence of the moving vehicle. Michael wondered if they could actually sense that they were not the prey.

The first day passed without an elephant sighting. Garrett patiently sat in the truck for over six hours, his eyes fixed on the overgrowth in front of him. He seemed mesmerized. When the guides said it was almost dusk and they needed to return to the compound, he became irritated and spoke to them in a harsh tone.

Later that evening as they ate dinner, Michael said, "I think I'm going to pass on tomorrow's trek. After today I think elephant hunting in too intense for me, but I'd like to get some pictures while I'm here. I'll get a guide to take me out."

Without looking up from his plate, Garrett spoke in a stern voice." You will go with us tomorrow, Mr. Charpelli. This isn't a vacation it's a safari." Michael could tell by the tone of his voice that this was not a request but an order.

After Garrett had gone to bed, Elliott and Michael sat outside on the screened veranda. "Man, listen to that sound," Elliott said. The air was filled with a droning hum from the insects flying around the lights. Night birds called to each other and occasionally a grunt or muffled roar could be heard in the distance. "This is an awesome place, but I hadn't planned on coming here with a dictator. Your father is something else," Michael said.

"Yeah, he sure likes to run the show. I think he was surprised when you talked back to him the other night. He's not used to being challenged." Elliott pulled a plastic baggy and a pack of papers out of his pocket. He rolled two joints and handed one to Michael. Michael bent over and cupped his hand while the flame touched the end of the paper. He took in a long drag. "Man, he sure is hell bent on getting an elephant.

Elliott laughed, "Not any elephant, Michael. There is one in particular he wants. It's a big bull with a white spot on his ear. He is huge. My old man went after him a few years back, but it got away. He was furious for days. It wasn't a pretty sight. You can only get a permit to hunt elephants every few years. You got two days and if you don't get one, it's over. He's been seen in this part of the country the last several weeks, so tomorrow is the big day. He has to get that elephant."

Michael leaned back in the chair and enjoyed the feeling of euphoria that had come over him. "I guess when you have as much money as your dad you got to find something that's a challenge."

The day dawned in a gray haze. By seven a.m. the air was already filled with stifling heat. Against Garrett's orders, Michael stayed behind at the encampment saying that he did not feel good.

"Your friend doesn't follow orders very well, does he?" Garrett said to Elliott. "I would have expected better of him, but I guess he is not up to the sight of an elephant kill. Too bad, he doesn't know what he is missing."

Garrett and Elliott once again made the trek out to the Savannah. After a monotonous two hours of the same scenery one of the guides stood up and pointed to the left of the truck. He began to speak in his native tongue, pointing at the herd of elephants that were now in view. Elliott grabbed his field glasses and watched as a group of males circled the herd, sometimes stopping to mount a cow, which would either stand still or thrash about. "Hey, looks to me, like the boys are trying to get some. Must be mating season," Elliot said.

"Different cows come in heat at different times, so that is why the bulls are never too far away." Garrett said. A loud bellow from the distance signaled that a larger and older male was entering the territory and wanted to announce his presence. "It's him! Look at him! He is a magnificent specimen. I can't believe I have another chance at him. We need to keep him in our sight. Don't lose him," Garrett ordered the guides.

Garrett continued to watch him through his field glasses. "Enjoy yourself, old boy. It won't be long before you're on my wall."

As the herd began to meander toward the shade of the trees, the driver slowly moved along with them at a safe distance with all eyes trained on the bull. The large elephant stayed behind for a while and then began to veer off into the thicket passing the herd of females. Smelling the scent of the fresh blood from the puncture wound the bull had received in his earlier confrontation one of the older females followed him into the brush to make sure he had not received a mortal blow.

"There he is! There he is!" Garrett whispered. His body tensed with sheer excitement. "Clear me a spot. I want to hit his side. I don't want to damage his head." He peered into the scope of his rifle, his heart pounding with the anticipation of downing the elephant.

"You need to wait until you can get a clear shot, Massa," the guide said, touching Garrett's arm.

Garrett shook clear of him and when the huge, gray back of the elephant appeared in the clearing, he squeezed the trigger twice on the .700 Nitro Express rifle. The elephant staggered out of the bush and fell to the ground. The thundering sound of the other plains animals running for their lives temporarily interrupted Garrett's pleasure from the kill. As the dust began to settle, he had a clear view of the elephant lying on the ground.

"God dammit! That's not him. Where in the hell did this one come from?" Garrett swore angrily. "Move! Maybe we can catch up with him, move!"

"No!" the guide yelled. "You already killed one elephant. That is your limit."

Garrett and Elliott jumped from the truck and walked over to her body. She was an old cow. Her left tusk was completely broken off and her ears had been shredded from years of living in the thorny bushes. The color of her hide had faded, leaving large patches of a deep pink layer of skin. She was by no means a prize specimen—at least not to Garrett.

"Son of a bitch. Look at this old thing. Take me back to the lodge. I've had it."

Garrett had no idea that he was now in the sights of the bull elephant that stood watching from a safe distance.

Still hidden in the thicket, Jakuta stared into the faces of the two men standing over the body of his mother. He studied their eyes, the sound of their voices, and the smell of their clothes. He would not forget these men. He had seen one of them before. The man had tracked Jakuta into the bush the year before, but he had eluded him when the thorns of the acacia trees were too fierce for the man to follow. Jakuta waited silently and patiently until the men got back into the truck and left.

Bayanni lay on her side. Ever so slowly she would lower her mud encrusted lashes to cover her eyes that were blinded by the sun. A row of bullet holes crossed her back, each one seeping blood on to the hard-packed ground of the Savannah. The heat waves formed a mirage behind her making the other elephants that had scattered when they heard the sound of gunfire, barely visible. Jakuta stood in the thicket watching as his mother lay dying. His head thrashed from side to side as he raised his trunk and let out a mournful bellow alerting the herd that it was too dangerous to come near her. The enemy was still present. The vultures were already beginning to swoop low over her body and soon the Savannah scavengers would smell the scent of death and a free meal. She would be enclosed in the circle of prey.

When the sound of the truck could no longer be heard, Jakuta walked toward his mother. He lowered his head and touched her back with his trunk. He walked around her, trying to kick the red clay over her, but it was useless. Within a few minutes the rest of the herd arrived. Small sounds, almost a whimper came from some, while the dust on the faces of others turned to mud as they cried. They would stay by her side until her scent had attracted too many predictors for them to fend off. They had to protect their calves. Jakuta raised his head and pawed at the ground still vibrating from the departing truck. He did not stay with the rest of the heard. After a few hours he left with crystal clear images imbedded in his head.

Bayanni's sister, Yemaya was now the matriarch of the herd.

"I'm telling you, Dad, Garrett Ferrell is a nut case. There was something about the look in his eye and the way he stroked his gun that made me almost afraid to be near him."

"Don't say that, Michael," Frank said. "Garrett is a brilliant man. It's just that I have heard he has a bad temper."

"Bad temper? Is that what you call it when somebody goes into a rage and throws his five-thousand dollar rifle in the fountain and knocks all the glasses off the bar. He cursed all of the guides and told them they he was going to have every one of them fired. Then he turned on Elliott and for a minute I thought he was going to hit him. He never spoke a word to either of us all the way home. I call that a nut case. He was so upset about that elephant that we stayed clear of him. Man, I don't care if I ever see him again."

"He is my employer, Michael. He provides our living and he is the father of your friend. Try to understand him."

Michael would try for his father's sake, but the nagging feeling in the back of his mind made him uneasy.

Alone in the forest, Jakuta filled his body with the fresh foliage on the blossoming trees. He had been away from the herd for almost two weeks and enjoying the peaceful, spring away from the chaos of the young bulls fighting for dominance on the fringe of the herd of females. He knew he need only converge on them and his presence would surely scatter them in all directions. For now he would keep his distance and gather strength for the months to come.

Chapter Nine

As each month passed Frank began to doubt himself. He was not sure that he had made the right decision moving to the corporate floor. He found the environment almost too sterile for him and impossible to penetrate. Each morning when he arrived at work he was greeted with a nod or a short hello from his fellow workers. The rest of the day was spent in the confines of his office with little or no communication with anyone but Carol. The silence was broken only by the soft music from the intercom system in the hallway. He occasionally looked outside his door to see if there was anyone to talk with. Frank had asked several of the other men out to lunch, which they declined. Even in the monthly business meeting in the convention room, small conversation was kept to a minimum. As soon as the meetings ended none of the men lingered for small talk, but scurried back to their offices. When Frank approached some of the married men about introducing his wife to their wives, they smiled and gave excuses, always politely refusing his invitations. The position was not at all what he had anticipated. He thought he would be involved in corporate decisions with the other corporate men and have meetings with clients. Maybe even travel a bit. Was he the problem and if so, why was he hired for this position? He would talk to Mr. Ferrell.

Frank decided it was time to tell Carol to arrange a personal meeting for him with Mr. Ferrell. "Are you going to give your resignation? Perhaps it may be a good idea if this position is causing you a great deal of stress. You know these types of jobs aren't for everyone."

Frank was annoyed. "I know I can handle this job. I just need to talk to Mr. Ferrell. Just arrange a meeting with him." He had never been sharp with her and a few minutes later apologized. He was scheduled to see Garrett at four that afternoon.

Garrett stood at the window with his hands clasped behind his back. Frank was shown into his office and stood in front of the desk, waiting for the signal to be seated. It came in the form of a small nod.

"Are you happy with my work, Mr. Ferrell?" Frank asked.

"Of course, Frank. Why do you ask?"

"I have found it somewhat difficult to understand why no one on this floor seems to have any personal contact with each other, not even lunch together or a drink after work. I am beginning to get a complex. I am still finding it strange that I do not even get to communicate with my clients other than through the computer. It would be nice to meet the heads of some of these companies I do business with or at least talk to them on the telephone. After all, I am moving millions of dollars around every day."

Garrett sat down and leaned back in his chair. "I have been wondering how long it was going to take for you to come to me. I am surprised it took this long. Let me tell you my position on corporate level business. You see, Frank, when you have nothing to lose you can throw caution to the wind. It's only when you start to become successful that every move you make must be calculated. I cannot afford to make mistakes, Frank. Wealthy people are put under the microscope and every thing you do becomes news. I have been the head of this enterprise for the last twenty years and I have made a few mistakes, but each time I do, I tell myself it will never happen again." Garrett paused. "Are you following me, Frank?" he asked.

"Somewhat, but…"

Garrett put up his hand. "Let me go on. It may become clearer. Of course you are aware that we are running a billion dollar operation and growing every year. We deal with countries that other companies won't touch. We have shipping lines, which you well know about, pharmaceutical interests, and financial dealings that change at a moment's notice. I cannot and will not have to worry about social graces and cocktail parties. I do not need my main line of defense conversing in the hallways. These practices may be acceptable on the lower floors and that is fine with me, but here…" Garrett tapped his finger on his desk, "We are all about business—business done my way. Everyone on this floor makes a tremendous salary with more than enough perks. If you are willing to work on those terms, then do so, if not, it is best that you move on. Have I made myself clear?"

Frank was slightly shocked by his sharp candor. There was nothing to say except, "I understand completely, Mr. Ferrell."

Garrett smiled. "Good, then do you want to stay on the floor or leave right away?"

"I'm staying," Frank answered.

"So you had a talk with your boss today, Frank. What did he say? Am I going to meet some of the wives? I could plan a meal, a nice meal and have them all over. We haven't entertained in such a long time. This big house just sits here with no one to even see it." Rosa was excited at the prospect of visitors in her home. "Maybe an Italian meal—I could make cannoles for dessert." Rosa seemed to be thinking out loud.

"I don't think so, Rosa. We need to find friends outside of work. We could join the country club or you could do some volunteer work at the hospital. I have good vacation time, we will travel, maybe go home to Italy."

"They don't want to come here, Frank, do they?" Rosa asked, her face suddenly losing its animation.

"It has nothing to do with you, Rosa it's just that they don't socialize with one another. It is too complicated for me to explain." Frank pulled at his tie. I'm tired. I think I'll go to bed early."

As the days lingered on, the nagging feeling that something was going on that he was unaware of kept creeping into his mind. There were meetings he was not involved in and new accounts appearing in his portfolio at an alarming rate. Overseas companies were transferring large amounts of money into the investment companies owned by Ferrell. But why—that was the question Frank wanted answered and the question no one wanted to answer for him. Today an even bigger mystery confronted him. One of the shipping lines was showing a deficit of fifty million dollars and the Ferrell account had increased by fifty million. He could not understand how that could have happened with no invoices and proof of purchases. He would have to find out and quickly.

Frank opened the door to Ari's office unannounced. He had waited for Ari's secretary to leave for lunch. "You busy?" he asked.

Ari looked up from his computer. He was startled. Turning off the screen he said, "Frank, is something wrong? Is it important?"

"I need to talk to you, Ari. Yes, it's important. It's about one of my accounts. My figures are way off."

Ari hurriedly scribbled four words on the notepad lying on his desk and pushed it in front of Frank. *Don't say anything else.*

"Okay, I'll be glad to take a look at it and see what is going on. Let's go see what it is." He took Frank by the arm and led him out of the office. As they stepped into the hallway, Ari whispered, "Go along with me, Frank. What ever I say, go along with me."

Bending over Frank's computer, Ari stared at the screen of numbers. "Here it is, Frank. Right here, you seem to have transposed these numbers." His hand squeezed Frank's arm.

"Oh, you're right. I sure did," Frank mumbled." That was a dumb mistake. I'm glad you found it. Thanks Ari. How could I make such a dumb mistake?"

Ari stood up. "Glad to be of help." He quickly left.

Frank stared at the screen once again. It wasn't his mistake. He was sure of it. Why were there so many misplaced decimal points in the accounts coming across his desk, especially from an account that he had never seen before?

Completely confused by what had just happened, Frank somehow had the instinct to know that he better leave things the way they were today until he could get to the bottom of it. Flipping back and forth between accounts Frank saw the numbers changing at a rapid pace. Someone was entering a large amount of data into one of his international accounts. According to what he could figure out, fifty million dollars had been withdrawn from an overseas investment company and transferred into the firm's bank. There was no record of a transaction of any kind in his previous ledger. What had the company bought from Ferrell in the last day? He was supposed to be responsible for this account. It just didn't make sense. And why had Ari been so secretive? It was as if he was afraid his actions were being watched. Another mystery added to Frank's already confused state.

Calling Carol into his office, he showed her the report and asked her if she knew anything about the transaction.

"Oh, *that* account. I understand that we are no longer doing business with them. They must be selling off their inventory to pay off their outstanding debt to our company. I can't imagine why it's still showing up on your computer."

"No one told me this company was no longer doing business with us. This is a very disturbing matter, Carol. This is a big loss for us and I'm still not sure where the fifty million came from and what is it for? I have no record of them being in arrears. Actually, I think I should go right to Mr. Ferrell with this information."

"No!" she said so loud it startled him. "He knows all about it. It was just an oversight that you were not notified that we were no longer doing business with them."

"I still would like to talk to Mr. Ferrell about this matter."

"I said…I would take care of it."

Frank was now agitated. "Do you mean just like the other errors I have shown you? Have you taken care of them, too?" Frank stood up. "Here, take my seat, obviously you know more about these accounts than I do."

"I'm sorry, Mr. Charpelli, I didn't mean to be so brisk with you." She seemed contrite and at a loss for words. "It's just that that sometimes these situations are not easily explained."

"Get me the telephone number of the bank in Pakistan that sent this money. I will talk to them directly."

"I'll call them…if you like, tomorrow. The banks in Pakistan are closed at this time of day," she said, meekly.

Frank rubbed his forehead. "I am very tired. We'll take care of this tomorrow. Have the number on my desk in the morning."

The next day Frank found a note on his desk that she had given the file to Herbert David, one of the other associates and he was going to take care of it. She said once again that Garrett was aware of the problem and that Frank was not to worry about it. Frank was vexed but had no other recourse than to drop the matter. Evidently Garrett did not feel he was capable of taking care of the account closure. He would have to find a way to broach the subject with Garrett since every time he approached Ari, he was told that it was all taken care of and none of his concern.

A few weeks later, Mr. David left the company. Frank arrived at work one morning to find that Mr. David's office was empty and was given the explanation that Herbert was not in good health and decided to retire. That made no sense at all to Frank. No mention was made of why Herbert would leave without saying goodbye to anyone and not even a small retirement reception to see him off. When he asked if he could have Herbert's address so that he could at least send him a card he was told that Mr. David had moved out of state. Even Carol seemed surprised at Herbert's quick exit from the company.

Frank decided to delve into the matter on his own. It would be his secret. He would not tell Carol or Ari or Mr. Ferrell that he was investigating the matter until he found positive proof to present to them. He wasn't satisfied with the incomplete and unconvincing answers he was given.

Each day when he arrived he would turn on his computer and instead of working on the transactions he was to complete for the day he began a search every account in his portfolio, trying to track as many of the transactions as he possibly could. He didn't care how long it took. With his only ally, Ari, gone off to Florida to take care of his ailing mother, he knew it was not going to be easy. He had called the number Carol provided for him five or six times, each time getting the same answering machine telling him to leave a message. What kind of bank used an answering machine?

After four weeks of trying to solve the mystery Frank gave up. He was ignoring his other accounts and had to work late each night to keep up with the flow of enormous work crossing his desk. Maybe he was just paranoid. Maybe everything was exactly as Garrett said it was, just maybe…

Jakuta roamed the bush and plains of the Savannah with the same cycle as the rest of the herd, yet he never associated with the other bachelor elephants or revisited the older female elephants that had been his baby-sitters while he was growing up. He stayed to himself except when the smell of a female in season became strong enough to draw him back to the herd. Jakuta was young, but he was not afraid to challenge the older bulls. He had grown large and strong over the years. His senses had grown keen, making him acutely aware when trouble approached. He was known to some of the tribes as a rogue elephant with the white ear since he demonstrated aggression to all those who came within his range, sometimes standing his ground he forced vehicles off the road. Yet he had not made an attack on a human or invaded a village.

Whenever Jakuta came upon the remains of a dead elephant, left by some poacher or hunter, he would circle it, pawing at the ground and sending out low sounds that could be heard as far away as five miles. He let it be known that killing one of his species was not acceptable and could be revenged.

Chapter Ten

Frank had now been working on the nineteenth floor over a year. He had complied with Garrett's wishes and become another one of the puppets with the strings being pulled by the master. Although his relationship with Carol had not improved he was now working with her on a daily basis. They bucked heads quite often and her reply was always the same, "Why don't you just resign, Mr. Chapelli?" Frank imagined that Carol wanted his position and if he resigned it would be given to her. Why else would she constantly be telling him to quit?

Frank knew without this job he would have to sell the house and would be unable to pay the enormous tuition payments to Michael's school. Why was it so important to him to bend to Ferrell's wishes? His relationship with Mr. Ferrell seemed to reconcile and his daily duties had become routine. He received a generous bonus that added to his already ample salary. His expenses seemed to be growing twice as fast as his bank account. Frank had no idea it would cost so much to live on Long Island. His mortgage and his taxes were exorbitant in addition to the cost of having a gardener and handy man working for him. It was costing a small fortune to keep Michael in his upscale apartment close to school, plus the tuition at Princeton. Against Michael's protest, Rosa insisted that Michael have a new car and generous allowance while he was away at school. Rosa was also racking up large amounts on her own credit card. With Michael away at school, Frank away at the office and no friends in the neighborhood, Rosa filled her hours watching the home shopping network. Each day parcels would be delivered to the house. Some of them she never opened. Her huge walk-in closet began to take on the appearance of a small store. She also made several pilgrimages to the Sisters of Mercy in Rome, each time taking them a large donation. Frank did not have the heart to tell her that she really needed to temper her spending habits.

Frank was still attentive to Rosa, occasionally taking her to dinner and Broadway shows. Yet, she was lonely in a way she had never been before and the sadness showed in her eyes. She talked about the old days when they lived in Flushing and how she wished she could go back there. "We have no friends, Frank. Even the wives of the men you used to work with have stopped calling me and when I call them they are always busy. I wonder what they do with their time?" There was nothing she wanted more than her husband and her old life back. She wanted the man that used to laugh and enjoy his dinner with her each night. Now he picked at his food, hardly talking during the meal and always going to bed early. So what was it all good for? The enormous salary and all the perks were supposed to make him happy. It wasn't doing *its* job. There were still too many inconsistencies in the position. He felt there was an ominous undercurrent that was going to pull him into the deep, black water at any time. The policy of don't ask became more and more prevalent.

After a long week at work, Frank sat down on the sofa next to Rosa. He took her hand. "I love you, Rosa. I love you more than you know, and Michael, too. I wish he were home right now. You are the most important people in my life."

Rosa looked at him quizzically. "Are you sick, Frank? What's wrong? You look so sad."

Frank rubbed his head. "I'm just tired. It's been a long week.

Rosa snuggled closed to him. "You're always tired," she said.

Later that night as he lay in bed, Frank stared into the dark. Where had he gone wrong? He had worked hard, proven himself and now he felt as though he was no longer in charge of his life. Had his vision been so tunneled that he never looked to the right or the left to see if there was something better out there for him? He was rich now, in debt and miserable. He had an ominous feeling that something was going on at his work that was out of his control. Something chilling that may cause him more trouble than he could imagine. In the past he had always been proud of working at Ferrell Enterprises. When he worked on the lower floors there were good people and also people in line who wanted his position. There were good people to share the workday with. They had birthday parties in the lounge and Christmas parties with Rosa always making special food for them. There were barbecues in the backyard and friendly card games. He had always had a good team.

Garrett Ferrell was completely different than he had imagined. Garrett's picture was always in the paper. He was always smiling that charismatic smile that Frank was sure Garrett had practiced to win people's admiration. With his silver gray hair and piercing blues eyes, he was a striking figure. Garrett was the benefactor for many institutions, giving millions of dollars to hospitals and universities. He seemed so nice when Frank first met him, but now Frank was convinced that Garrett had a dark side, much more threatening than he knew. He remembered what Michael had said about him after the safari. It had upset him at the time, but now he wasn't too sure that Michael wasn't right after all.

"Rosa, Rosa, wake up," he said, lightly shaking her shoulder. Rosa turned and sat up. "I have come to a decision, Rosa. I am going to talk to Mr. Ferrell tomorrow about transferring me to another department. We can reclaim our old life. Maybe we will even look into buying a house in our old neighborhood. This place is much too big for us."

Rosa threw her arms around his neck. “Thank you, Frank. Oh, thank you. I would love it so much.” They sat up for a couple of hours talking. When Frank finally went back to bed, he had a peaceful night’s sleep for the first time in months.

Jakuta had entered dangerous ground. The rains had brought pools of mud that were sometimes difficult to navigate. Losing his footing could also mean losing his life. If he were to get mired down in the thick sludge, it would be difficult to get out. Lions were on the prowl around the peripheral of the quagmire waiting patiently for just such an accident by one of the plains animals. A full-grown elephant is an unlikely prey for lions, but a pride of eight or nine could take him on if he were down.

Jakuta struggled across the murky swamp to the dry ground on the other side. Others were not so lucky. He could hear the brays of the wildebeests as the lions closed in. He could not be concerned with their plight. He had a quest of his own.

Chapter Eleven

It took a few days before Frank was able to set up a meeting with Garrett. Frank was nervous. He had the distinct feeling that Garrett was avoiding him. He did not want Garrett to think that he had made a bad choice by choosing him for this position. Frank was going to take all the blame for wanting to change positions.

"Come in, Frank," Garrett said. "I'm sorry I couldn't get to you sooner. It's been a busy time for me. What can I do for you?"

Frank cleared this throat. "Mr. Ferrell, I want to let you know that I have enjoyed working in the corporate office, but I feel that perhaps I was hasty in taking the position and I…well, I have decided I would like to give up my office and if possible direct my attention in another avenue in this company." He had practiced this speech over and over.

"Frank, Frank, what am I going to do with you? We've had this conversation before. I have been pleased with your work. What could have possibly changed your mind about your position?" Garrett said in a condescending tone.

"To be honest with you, there are quite a few things. Some not worth mentioning at this time, but the one that disturbs me the most is the fact that I have little or no control over the accounts in my portfolio. I still feel that if I could talk to some of these companies face to face I may be able to make better decisions when it comes to transferring their money into different financial plans. Then there is still the nagging problem I had with the mysterious fifty million dollars. It was passed off as if it was not important. I have asked about it several times and have been given only vague responses to its disposition. I can't help it. It still concerns me. What kind of company gets fifty million dollars from an unknown source then loses it in the system. I am a precise person, Mr. Ferrell. I want to do a good job, but I don't feel like I have any free range. I get a list of accounts to take care of everyday and that is it. Almost anyone in this company could be doing what I am doing right now."

"Do I pay you well, Frank?" Garrett asked.

"Of course."

"Do you need a raise?"

"No. I'm not here to talk about money. I'm here to talk about this company and how I can get some answers and why is it I can never talk to anyone on the telephone or meet with them in person? What would be the harm? Surely some of these companies would appreciate a face to face meeting." Frank asked.

Garrett stood up and leaned against the front of his desk just inches from Frank. "I don't understand why you are still harping on something that happened months ago. The account was closed. The error was found. End of story, Frank. It was a costly fifty million dollar mistake, but it will never happen again. When you get to the level you are on now, you have to follow orders. There is no room for anyone changing the rules. It works, Frank. Trust me it works. I don't want you to leave right now. Stay a while longer and see if things don't improve for you and if they don't I'll make sure I find a place that is best for both of us. Is that a deal?" Garrett said, smiling.

He wanted to say no. He wanted to say I quit and walk out. Yet there was something about the commanding tone and glaring look from Garrett that made him melt in his chair. "I suppose I can do that. I will just say one more thing about that matter and then I will leave it go. I really think we may need to get the banking authorities involved in this one. It may be some sort of a scam."

"I don't think that will be necessary, Frank. Just as soon as you leave I am going to make a complete investigation into the problem. Now go back to work and have a good day."

As Frank left the office, Garrett's face turned to an angry frown. He picked up his phone and dialed a single number. "I have something I want you to take care of. Now!"

Frank was annoyed that the meeting hadn't gone as he expected. He wanted out but he had been too much of a coward to state his position and stick to it. He dreaded telling Rosa. She was so happy that morning. He would take her to dinner tonight and break the news.

When Frank arrived home, Rosa met him at the door. "Let me take you out to dinner tonight," he said, before she could ask him any questions.

"That would be good. I'll go change." Rosa started up the stairs and then stopped. "There is an envelope for you on the hall table. A courier brought it just a few minutes ago."

Frank tore the flap on the brown wrapper and pulled out the contents. Two white envelopes fell out. He opened the first.

Frank,

I wanted to let you know that I appreciate your concern for my company. I have the matter under advisement and I'm sure it will be settled soon. You are a valued employee and you need to be rewarded for your diligence.

Garrett Ferrell

Frank was pleasantly surprised that Garrett would send him a personal note. He opened the second envelope and pulled out a check. He recognized the company logo. The check was made out to him, with the word bonus written on it.

"Oh my God!" Frank said out loud. His hand was shaking. The check was for three hundred thousand dollars. Frank walked into the living room and sat down. He looked at the numbers again. Was this the pay off for diligence or a pay off to keep quiet? He ran his fingers over the numbers on the check. Should he keep it?

After telling Rosa of his decision to stay on at Ferrell a while longer and thinking about the check, Frank had another sleepless night. He had once again disappointed his wife in favor of Ferrell Enterprises.

The following day, Frank gave Carol the check in a sealed envelope and told her to return it to Mr. Ferrell. "Please tell him that I appreciate his generosity, but there is no way I can accept this."

Carol held the envelope in her hand. "If this is your bonus check and you are returning it, Mr. Ferrell will be greatly offended. He prides himself in giving bonuses to his employees."

"You don't understand, Carol. This is a very…I mean

very large amount. Much more than a bonus check should ever be."

"You don't have to return it. I'll take care of it, Mr. Charpelli. Why don't you let me deposit it in an account for you and you can decide what you want to do with it later. You need to make sure your funds are safe."

Her eyes traveled around the room knowing that the office was wired for sound. She wanted to scream at him, *take the money, Frank, take the money and run. Run as fast and as far away from here as you possibly can.* It was happening again. Very soon the quick sand called Ferrell Enterprises would swallow Frank Charpelli. She had to warn him. It would not be easy.

Frank was surprised by her response. It almost seemed that she wanted to protect him in some way. He was probably just imagining it.

The rain had come again. At first a blessing, cooling his skin and washing away the months of debris that had collected on his hide. As the days lingered on with more and more torrents of rain, a sense of irritation began to creep into his being. He wished for it to end.

Chapter Twelve

A month had passed and Frank was even more miserable at work. More and more accounts began to show up on his ledgers with large amounts of money going in and out on a daily basis. He now had an international shipping company account to take care of. It was difficult to keep up with his workload. It was almost as if the enormous amount of work was meant to keep him so busy he did not have time to think about anything else.

Arriving at work on a Monday morning, he hung his wet overcoat and umbrella on the coat tree. He walked to his window and watched the rain pelt down on the sea of black umbrellas moving along the sidewalk. He wished he were one of them. Going anyplace but to this miserable office.

Sitting down at his desk he noticed a small slip of paper peaking out from under the mouse pad. It was a typed note with no name on it. "*Use this as your entry code today. Highly confidential information and for your eyes only. Destroy this paper as soon as you know the code. Record all the information from the screen on to paper.*" Was this some kind of test or joke? He didn't have time to deal with it. He stuffed the paper into his pocket and went on with his daily routine. Surely someone would come into his office and explain what this was all about. No one ever did.

At the end of the day, Frank put the paper into his briefcase. He walked slowly to his car. The ringing of his cell phone interrupted his thoughts.

"Hey, Pop, how are you?" Michael asked. "I haven't heard from you in quite a while."

"Hello, Son, it's good to hear your voice. I'm fine. I've just been busy and how are you?"

"I talked to Mom the other day and she said she is worried about you. She said you hardly eat or sleep and she thinks you look sick. What's going on? Do you want me to come home?"

"Michael, you know your mother, she worries about every little thing. It's just my job."

"Well, why don't you quit?" Michael said, laughing. "You got enough money to live on. Besides this is my last year in school and then you'll get a real break on my expenses. Maybe I can even start giving you money."

"I may just do that, Michael. I just might quit. I'm going to have to hang up now. I'm getting on the expressway. You study hard, but take time to enjoy yourself, you hear. Life is too short. I want you to always remember that if something happens to me you are to take care of your mother. Make sure she has a happy life," Frank said. "No matter what happens, you remember that your father loves you very much."

"Now, you really got me worried, Dad. What's wrong?"

'Nothing is wrong, Michael. I just wanted to tell you those things. They have been on my mind."

Michael was puzzled by their conversation. His father seemed so dejected. He must be sick. He would have to try and get home before the end of the semester.

The next morning Carol entered Frank's office carrying two cups of coffee. Frank looked up from his computer. She smiled at him. Something she rarely did. " I brought you coffee." Something else she had never done. How are you today, Frank? It's a beautiful day. Might be a nice weekend to get away somewhere. I'm going to stay in and just relax. I rented some old James Bond movies. My favorite is For Your Eyes Only. Did you ever hear of it, Frank?" She stared into his face with a knowing look. 'You really should rent it sometime. It is a very good movie."

The words jumped out at him. For your eyes only—she was sending him a message. Those were the words on the note. She stared at him, her eyes pleading with him not to say the wrong thing.

"That may be a good idea, Carol." He smiled back at her. What was she trying to tell him? Why would she have given him some illusive code? Before he barely finished his sentence she turned and left his office.

Frank opened his briefcase and retrieved the crumpled up piece of paper. He entered the code and then waited.

The screen went blue for a few seconds and then rows of names and numbers began to appear before him. Some of the names he recognized. Others he had never seen. There were transactions where large sums of money were entered into the Ferrell accounts and then even larger amounts withdrawn and sent to banks all over the world. There were invoices for purchases that Frank had never seen. Thousands of Persian rugs, loose gem stones and gold ingots were part of the stock on the invoices. Ferrell represented none of these companies. It took only a few minutes for Frank to realize that his suspicions that something in the company was highly irregular were true. Garrett was involved in an international money-laundering scheme. It was highly sophisticated and complex. Frank was stunned realizing that for the last year he was supplying money to these companies. He pulled out a stack of blank paper and began writing everything down.

Carol returned a few hours later and gave Frank a knowing glance. She placed a stack of folders on his desk. One folder was tagged with a red post-it. As soon as she left, he flipped opened the pages of the file. Another small note in Carol's precise handwriting:

Your every move is being monitored. Keep the papers in a safe place. I want you to look at your personal account and tell me where you would like to transfer the money that Garrett has set up. It will be used to blackmail you. We must get rid of it. You must and I repeat must have leverage. Your life is in danger.

Frank stared at the bank statement she had laid in front of him. Where did the account come from? That name of the bank was foreign to him. The statement had his name on it and showed the balance in the account was twenty seven million dollars. He said the amount over and over in his head. How could that be? The only time he had made a deposit in an overseas bank was when he got the large bonus. He had withdrawn that money months ago to pay off some of his debt. His hands trembled. He had to get to the bottom of this and quickly. He scribbled a message on a piece of paper and buzzed Carol. She was in his office in a second. She glanced down at the paper on his desk. *What should I do?"*

"Well, Mr. Charpelli I think I can take care of this for you. I will work on it right now and bring the file back to you." She picked up the bank statement and once again returned to her own office.

The hours ticked away slowly as Frank tried to concentrate on the work he was supposed to be doing. Now that he knew *what* he was doing, his fingers seemed numb as he entered the day's transaction into the computer.

By the end of the day Carol put a file folder in front of him. She held it closed with her hand. "Here is the information you need, Mr. Charpelli. It should be helpful to you." Another post-it on the front of it read: *take this home with you. Keep it in a safe place.*

Frank now had a new bank account with the First Federal Savings & Loan in Los Angeles, California. It was under the name of Jackson Brown. Still confused he was too tired to even think what this meant. He turned off the light in his office and headed for the safety of the outside world.

Frank opened the door to the Quick Mart and stepped inside. Just as he started down the aisle he heard someone call his name. He turned to see Ari Goldman coming in behind him. It was the first time he had seen Ari in weeks. "Hello, Ari, when did you get back from Florida? How is your mother?" Frank asked.

"I got back today. She's fine. It took her a while to recover from her stroke, but she is doing okay. How is everything going at work?"

Frank frowned, "That's a long story. By the way, what are you doing in this neighborhood, I thought you lived downtown."

"My sister lives not far from here. I just left her house. She was picking up my mail for me."

"I come in here almost every night and get ice cream for Rosa. She loves her ice cream." Frank didn't know what else to say.

"You look awfully tired, Frank, is everything okay?

"No, not really."

"Well, listen, there is a little café about two blocks down the street. I was going to stop in and get myself a sandwich. You want to go with me? We can talk."

"Uh…sure, I'll go. I'll call Rosa and tell her I'll be a little late."

In the dim light of the café, they drank their coffee while waiting for their order. "I'm thinking of quitting," Ari blurted out. "I can't handle all of the pressure. Everything seems to be getting out of hand in my department. I don't like the feeling I'm getting about the company. Something is going on that seems very suspicious to me. Garrett is getting more and more out of control and I think something really bad is going to happen soon."

Surprised by Ari's admission, without thinking Frank uttered, "I've been thinking about quitting, too. You and I are on the same page. I think there is something going on that I don't like either and…" Frank stopped, he was going to mention Carol's name, but decided he did not want to draw her any further into this chaos. "Can I tell you something in complete privacy, Ari? I do believe that Mr. Ferrell is running a money laundering scam with foreign companies. They are sending him huge amounts of money. He invests it and returns it to them all cleaned up. I have no idea how long this has been going on, but it is big, real big, Ari."

"Are you sure, Frank? This is shocking news."

"I have found a way to get into the accounts that are password protected. I have been copying down all of the information. I have names and governments and transactions that will put Mr. Ferrell out of business and in jail for a long time. I don't want to get caught in the middle of something illegal. I think you ought to protect yourself, Ari. Obviously he doesn't care what happens to us."

"Man, I knew something was going on, but I didn't expect anything as big as that. How did you manage to get into those files? I sure hope you're keeping that information in a safe place."

"I got in quite by accident. There was a glitch in my computer program and it flipped me into another screen." Frank patted the side of his suit coat. "I got the information right here in my pocket. You've been with the company for a while and so have the others. I can't believe I am the only one who was suspicious. Are you sure you never knew about it?"

"No. Come on, tell me the truth. You've had help with this, haven't you?"

"Maybe a little, but I don't want to get anyone else involved in this mess."

Ari rubbed his hand across his forehead. "I'm serious, I always knew we were connected to something bigger than Ferrell Enterprises but I had no idea it was illegal. I've never seen anything like that on my computer. Maybe it is all set up in your system. Listen, Frank, we got to be careful what we are doing. I got to tell you, Frank, the money has always been good. That's why I never said anything, but I know I'm about to inherit enough to get me out of that job. My mother is very ill. I think it would be best if you let me resign first. I can tell Garrett I need to go back to Florida. Then about a week from now you can give him your notice. That way nothing will seem suspicious. Once we are out of it, we can go to the authorities together. Until then you have to keep everything under wraps."

"You don't know how relieved I am to have you on my side, Ari. In the mean time, I'll see what else I can find out." They shook hands and left the café.

Frank sat on the edge of the bed taking off his shoes. "Did you have a good time with your friend?" Rosa asked.

"I'm sorry, I didn't mean to wake you. Yes, it was fine," Frank, replied.

She rubbed her hand across his back. "You know I can't sleep unless you are here beside me. I was just resting."

Frank took a hanger out of the closet and put his jacket on it. "I have some papers here that belong to the company, Rosa. I need to work on them at home, but I would like for you to keep them in a safe place. They are getting too bulky to carry around."

"Just put them in your dresser drawer. No one will bother them," Rosa said.

"No, I would rather you took them and put them away safe."

Rosa opened her nightstand and stuck the envelope between the pages of a photo album. She never questioned anything about his work, so there was no reason for her to ask him what they were.

The dry season had come again to the Savannah. Food was scarce and tempers short in the elephant herd. The bulls followed the herd across the cracked, red clay mile after mile. A single tree meant a few leaves to sustain them for a time. Jakuta barged into a group of young bulls already feeding on an almost stripped tree. Too weak to challenge him, they moved away. They were always looking for the fountain of life—water.

A few miles down the road an old bull stumbled and fell into the clearing. He was unable to get up. His time had come. When Jakuta came upon him, the bull was barely breathing. Jakuta put his trunk in the old bull's mouth. A sign of greeting that was seldom exchanged among males. A few minutes later the rest of the elephants arrived. It was difficult losing one of their own and even more difficult for them to make sense of it. They would stay for a while and mourn for him before moving on.

Chapter Thirteen

It was a grueling week. Frank's nerves were raw and for the first time in his married life he had been cross with Rosa. A few minutes later he told her how sorry he was for yelling at her over something very silly, but his mind was cluttered with irrational thoughts about his future. He wished he hadn't said anything to Ari. What if his suspicions were wrong? He would have involved an innocent man in the middle of it. A few days later he heard that Ari had resigned. He wondered how Garrett had taken the news of Ari's resignation. It seemed strange to him that someone as important to Garrett as Ari was could leave the company and nothing would be said about it.

Frank began counting down the days until he could leave also. He felt he had enough evidence to prove that Garrett was involved in a large-scale money laundering operation. Most of the purported companies did not exist and those that did were in countries not in favor with the American government.

Frank left the office at lunchtime and walked the streets of New York. The thoughts were whirling around in his head. He had to find a way to talk to Carol alone. Should he call Rosa and tell her to pack them a bag or maybe he should call Michael. He would finish up the day and then make his decision. He had to act normal, whatever normal was right now.

After lunch he returned to the building and unlocked the door to his office. He was startled to see Garrett sitting in his office.

"Mr. Ferrell, this is a surprise."

"We need to have a talk, Frank. Sit down," he said pointing to the chair in front of the desk. Frank slowly sank into the chair.

"I am disappointed in you, Frank. Very disappointed. I really thought that you would work out well in this position and now I find you are snooping into areas that are of no concern to you. You've made a good deal of money for me in the past year. I had hoped your time here would last much longer. But now what do I find out. I find that you are privileged to information that is not your concern. And…you have taken money from this company. My money, Frank. I want it back and I want the papers you're hiding.

"I deserve an explanation for what is going on around here. I think you know what I am talking about. I am an honest man, Mr. Ferrell. I have never been greedy."

Garrett laughed. "Honest? How does the word honest fit into the same sentence with the word greed? You, Frank, have always been a greedy man? You like your big house and fancy cars and buying presents for your wife, don't you, Frank? You like the idea that your son can attend a prestigious university."

"I wouldn't call that greedy. I have worked hard to get this position," Frank answered, angrily.

"There is one problem, Frank. You stepped across the line and when you did, you accepted the salary and all the perks. Do you really think you, Frank Charpelli; with your pitiful little bachelor's degree in accounting belong on this floor or any floor above the third? Of course not. You see, Frank, I hand picked you. I had been watching you for quite a few years before your promotion. I knew all about you. I was aware of how you pushed your people to do good, always telling them if they did well they would make more money. It was always about the money, wasn't it, Frank?"

"I was ambitious, everyone knew that. They all knew I had hopes of someday being wealthy. What about you, Mr. Ferrell? Why would anyone who has a company the size of yours want to do something illegal?"

The word *illegal* struck home. Garrett narrowed his eyes, his jaw tightened. "I am in charge," he said, raising his voice. "What I am doing is beneficial for all involved. I have put billions of dollars into this company and paid your salary. Someday I will have the largest multinational company on this continent."

"What is wrong with you Mr. Ferrell? Don't you have any morals?"

"Morals are for idiots. You only get one chance to make the best of it…the very best of it. After a point it is not only about the money. Money translates into numbers. The higher the number, the more power you have. Whether you're a bully in a schoolyard taking the other kids lunch money or the head of a government, it is always about the money and the power. I don't believe you understand that kind of logic. I have put up with you much longer than I should have only because of the friendship between our sons. I have been annoyed with you for a long time now. Your son will just have to deal with it. People like you are dispensable." He pushed a button on the corner of his desk. "Look around you, Frank. What do you see? Everything in this office spells money. My money! I took this threepenny company and turned it into a billion dollar operation. The truth is Frank; there is only one truth in business and that is everyone wants to be a winner. And I will do whatever it takes to win, even if it means stepping on those that get in the way."

Frank turned as the door opened. Ari Goldman and another large man that he did not know walked in.

"Ari! What are you doing here?" Frank was shocked to see him.

"I'm sorry, Frank. I wish things could have turned out differently."

Garrett walked from behind the desk. "Make sure that Frank gives you the papers and tells you where he has hidden the money," he said and left.

Frank's eyes darted from Ari to the other man. He supposed he was being escorted out of the building.

Howard grabbed Frank by his arms. He struggled as the two men led him down the hall and into his own office. Ari closed the door.

Ari pushed Frank into a chair. "Now, it's real simple. You trust me, don't you Frank? I am a man of my word. Just give me those papers and the whereabouts of the money and we can call it a day."

"And what if I do? What will happen to me then? I suppose you are going to tell me that you are going to let me walk right out of the building. I'll give you what you want when my wife and son are somewhere safe. Until then, you get nothing."

Howard grabbed the front of Frank's shirt and pulled him out of the chair. Frank kicked and pushed against him as he dragged him across the slick floor into the bathroom. Ari followed carrying a straight back office chair. "Nice tie, Frank. Italian silk, isn't it? They cost a pretty penny and they're strong." He slipped open the knot and pulled the tie off of Frank's neck. Standing on the chair he flipped the tie over the window rod and tied it into a knot. "Now, Frank, let's talk some more. If you give me what I want I will promise that your family will be safe, if not, well…" his eyes traveled up to the tie.

"How can you do this? Ari, I trusted you. You've let Garrett Ferrell turn you into criminals for his financial gain. Who do you think will go to jail when they find my body? Not Garrett. He will make sure it will be you two."

"Shut up!" Ari screamed. He nodded to Howard and they lifted Frank on to the chair. Howard grabbed the tie and put it around Frank's neck, pulling it tightly. Frank gasped for air. "This is your last chance, Charpelli. Where is it?"

Frank spit in his face. "Never, I will never tell you. You bastards will burn in hell. You will never get away with this."

Howard pulled the chair out from under Frank. Frank's body dropped downward, and stopped with a halting jerk. A stream of urine ran down the front of his pants and on to the floor. His eyes rolled back in his head as his head slumped forward.

"Jesus, Howard, you killed him. Dammit. We got nothing." He reached into Frank's jacket pocket hoping to find the papers. "Garrett is not going to like this one bit. Dammit." Ari stomped out of the office.

Howard wiped off his face with his handkerchief. "Nobody spits on me. Nobody."

Rosa was working in her flower garden when she heard the doorbell ring. She stood up and removed her gloves. As she cleared the side of the house Rosa saw the police car sitting in the driveway. Her heart sank. Something was wrong. Rushing up the porch stairs she called to the two men standing at her door. Both men wore black suits and mirrored sunglasses, their eyes hidden from view. "Yes, what is it?" she asked.

"Are you Mrs. Charpelli?" one of the men asked.

"Yes, I am, what is this about? Is it my son? Has there been an accident?" She was frantic.

"We need for you to come with us, Mrs. Charpelli," the other man said. "Yes, there has been an accident. It's your husband."

Rosa could feel her legs giving way under her. One of the men reached out and took her arm. They escorted her to the car and helped her in. The same man turned around and faced her. "I'm sorry, I can't give you any more information. We were just sent here to get you."

Rosa sat on the edge of the seat. She would wait. Right now she didn't want to know. She would wait and pray that it was only a small injury.

When the car turned into the hospital, it veered past the emergency room and drove down the narrow alley behind the building. She was helped out of the car and led down the side-walk leading to a single unmarked door. One of the men knocked on it and an attendant in a white, lab coat let them in.

"Mrs. Charpelli," the attendant said, "Is there anyone with you?"

"No, no, I'm alone. Please tell me what is wrong with Frank. Did he have a heart attack?"

"I hate to break the news to you by yourself, I wish there was someone here with you."

Rosa screamed. "You tell me what happened to Frank. Please take me to him right now."

The attendant touched her arm and said, "Wait here." Seconds later an older man came out of another door on the hallway. "Mrs. Charpelli, I am Detective McCabe. I am sorry, but your husband has committed suicide. He was found in the bathroom of his office. He hung himself."

She must have fainted. She was now looking up into the face of the detective and a doctor was taking her pulse. She tried to sit up.

"Please, lay still for a minute. If you sit up you are going to be dizzy," the doctor said. "I have prescribed a sedative for you, it should be here momentarily."

"Tell me what happened?" Rosa sobbed. "My Frank would never kill himself. No, not my Frank. Tell me what happened? My husband isn't dead. There must be some mistake," she moaned.

Detective McCabe took her hand. "I know this is a shock and it's all under investigation, but it appears to be a suicide. His secretary came back from lunch and he was not in his office. When she couldn't find him after a couple of hours, she pushed open the door to the bathroom and saw him hanging on the window bar. He had been dead for about four hours."

"No! No!" Rosa screamed. "Oh my God, my Frank, my poor Frank! I want to see him. Take me to him."

"Is there anyone I can call for you, Mrs. Charpelli?" the attendant asked.

"Yes, call my son. His name is Michael. He is at school. He goes to Princeton. Call him and tell him to come home right now." Rosa stood up. "Take me to my husband." The detective nodded and the attendant led her down the hall. He opened the door to the morgue. Rosa began to shiver. She held her arms tight to her body and watched as the attendant pulled a drawer out of the stainless steel wall. He pulled back the white sheet and stepped aside.

Her hands went to her face. She covered her mouth to keep from screaming. It was Frank. Her beloved Frank lay on the table. His face was a pale shade of gray. She could see the mark that circled his neck. Rosa ran her fingers through his hair and let the tears fall onto his chest. "Oh, Frank. Why did you do this ? Why? You know I cannot live without you. Why did you do this?" She was sobbing now. Heaving sobs that wracked her body. The attendant pulled the sheet up and pushed the drawer in. "Come, Mrs. Charpelli. Let me get you a cup of coffee."

"My husband, he is so cold. Feel his hands. They are like ice. Please get him a blanket," she said as she was led from the room.

Jakuta had been injured in a fight with another bull elephant. He had a large gash running down his side. The insects and birds were working on his wound and making him irritated. Rubbing his skin against the bark of a Djakarta tree would help to heal the wound. The thick sap seeping from the bark would coat his wound and give it time to mend. He would stay close to the tree for a few days and then go deeper into the bush. Jakuta wanted to be left alone. He was hurting. Not only his side, but also his pride was wounded. For the first time in his adult life he had lost a battle to a younger bull.

Chapter Fourteen

Michael opened the door to his mother's room. "Mom," he said, softly, adjusting his eyes to the darkness.

"Come in, Michael, but please don't turn on the lights."

Michael sat down on the side of the bed. "Oh, Mom, I can't hardly believe this is true. When that detective called me at school I thought it was a joke. I can't believe Dad did this. I knew he was a little depressed, but I had no idea it was that bad. What happened?" Michael choked back the sobs that had been heavy on his chest since he left school that afternoon.

Rosa took his hand. "I don't know. He seemed so distant lately. He would sit staring at the television, but I knew he wasn't watching it. I would ask him over and over to talk to me, but he wouldn't. He barely ate and I thought he was sick, but when I told him he needed to see a doctor, he said no and told me to leave him alone. My heart broke for him, but he wouldn't let me help him. We have lost him, Michael and I don't know how I am going to make it through each day." Michael put his arms around his mother and they sat in the dark crying for a man that they had both loved dearly and asking themselves how this could have happened.

The next day, Mr. Ferrell and Elliott came to the Charpelli house. Michael was trying to intervene on behalf of his mother since she was unable to control herself. Any mention of Frank's name sent her into bouts of crying.

"I can't tell you how sorry I am. I was shocked when I was given the news," Garrett said. "I called Elliott immediately so that he could be with you in your time of grief."

Elliott put his arm around Michael. "Man, this is awful. I wished I would have known sooner and I would have flown home with you. Is there anything I can do for you?"

"Not really. I've made all the arrangements. My mother wants a private funeral and no visitation at this time. We may plan to have a memorial service in a few weeks when we are both more in charge of our emotions. Right now, it is just too much to handle. I'm worried about her, too."

"I can certainly understand," Garrett said. "I want you to know if there is anything I can do for you and your mother I will be more than happy to oblige. He was a valued employee and a wonderful man. Everyone in the office sends condolences. I can't tell you how shocked we all are."

"Did my father seem different to you lately? I mean...did he seem depressed to you, Mr. Ferrell?"

"I did notice that he seemed unusually quiet and withdrawn from the rest of the staff. Several others on the floor had asked me if he was all right. I am so sorry I didn't pay more attention to the signs, perhaps I could have helped him, but when I asked him if anything was wrong, he always said no. I didn't feel it was my place as his employer to pry into his private life. What a shame. Everyone in the company will miss Frank. I have to leave now, but Elliott is going to stay for a while."

Around seven, Michael and Elliott ate dinner in the kitchen, Rosa still not wanting to come out of her room. "What are you going to do now, Michael?" Elliott asked.

"I don't know. You know my mom is never going to get over this. She is going to die of a broken heart. I can see it already. God, I feel so sorry for her. Maybe I can find her a place to live near the university. It's only three months to graduation. I have worked my ass off and I know this isn't really the time to say it, but I really want to graduate. Man, I still can't believe my dad actually killed himself. I am so pissed at him right now. He could have stayed alive for her. Depressed or not, he knew she needed him and so did I."

"People who commit suicide don't think about that kind of stuff. He must have really been in bad shape. I guess no one really knew how bad. Man, I've known your parents for years now and I sure can't figure this one out. He seemed like such a happy man and I was always so jealous of your relationship with him. You've got to know he loved you."

"It's hard for me to believe that right now. My dad was an open book, Elliott. He never hid anything, not even his feelings. If he had something to say, he said it. What could have changed all of that?"

"No one is really an open book, unless they've torn out a couple of pages. Nobody knows who we are, except ourselves.

Whoever your father was, he was in a lot of pain. Enough to block out all of his thoughts to relieve that pain."

"You really believe that?"

"I do," Elliott replied.

"He was my dad. I loved him so much and he loved us. He would never kill himself. He would never do that to my mom and me. I know something is not right and when I find out what really happened…" He couldn't finish his sentence. His body was wracked with sobs that sent him to his knees. He leaned against the chair and cried out, "Pop, oh Pop, why, why did this happen?"

Elliott bent down and put his arm around his friend. He knew there was nothing he could say to ease his pain.

Elliott spent a restless night thinking about Michael and his parents. He had never experienced that kind of love. At least Michael had that love growing up. Elliott had spent most of his life alone. There were times when he wished that Frank and Rosa were his parents. Now he realized that even the best of relationships could get torn apart in an instant.

The next day as Elliott prepared to leave he put his arm around Michael's shoulder. "I hate to do this to you Meatball, but I have to get back to school. I'm not on the dean's list like you are. I have to hit the books and cram for finals. Are you going to be okay?"

"Yeah, I'm just going to stay here until I am sure my mom is settled." He put his arm around Elliott's shoulder. "Thanks for staying. It has helped a lot."

"I want to say goodbye to your mom before I leave," Elliott said. "Can I go upstairs?"

Michael walked in front of him up the winding staircase and down the hallway to the closed door. He knocked lightly. "Mom, are you awake? Elliott wants to tell you goodbye."

"Come in," Rosa replied. She was sitting in a chair by the window, a photo album on her lap.

"I'll wait out here," Michael said.

Elliott walked over and knelt down before Rosa. "Mrs. Charpelli, I know there is nothing I can say to make you feel better, but I did want to tell you something. The way Michael talked about his father always made me jealous. Even though he is gone, you have some wonderful memories." He didn't want to say that it was more than he ever had in his life.

"Thank you, Elliott. You are a good friend to my son. She pointed to a small black and white picture in the book. See, here is a picture of Frank and I right after we got married. He was so handsome." A tear rolled down her cheek. She touched Elliott's hair as if he were a small boy. Rosa pulled out an envelope that was tucked between the front pages of the book. "Frank gave me these papers to keep for him just before he…well. I have them and I think they must have something to do with work. He would have wanted them returned to the office. Can I give them to you and you can take them to your father? I don't know if they are important, but maybe it is something he would want."

"Of course. Is there anything else I can do for you?"

"Yes, you make sure Michael goes back to school after the funeral. He needs to finish college. That would make his father very proud." The tears welled up in her eyes. Elliott kissed her on her cheek and left with the papers in his hand. He didn't open the envelope.

"Damn, I need a drink, in fact I need several drinks," Elliott said. "I just can't imagine what your mother is going through. I've never seen anyone filled with that much grief."

"I think I need a drink, too." Michael broke open a new bottle of Chavez and it was just about empty when Elliott got up to leave. "Are you okay to drive?" Michael asked.

"I'm fine. I'll see you tomorrow at the funeral," Elliott said, as he staggered to his car."

"Okay. Elliott there is one more thing…thanks for being here for me. It means a lot to me," Michael said, slurring his words. He was too drunk himself to know that Elliott should not have been driving.

"No problem, Meatball, you'd do the same for me." Elliott closed the car door. He reached over, almost falling off the seat and stuffed the brown envelope into the glove compartment.

Michael held his mother's arm as he led her down the aisle of the church. There was a large picture of Frank and a bouquet of white roses on the altar. Rosa genuflected and then slid into the pew. She knelt down, her head in her hands and prayed. She prayed that Frank would be allowed in heaven even though he took his own life. She prayed that she would join him soon. She prayed that Michael would forgive his father. Rosa sat down and glanced around the church. It was filled with people she hardly knew even though it was supposed to be a private service. People who had worked with Frank, neighbors who had never even bothered to say hello and a few old friends from Flushing came out of their love for Frank and Rosa. It didn't matter. Rosa was alone.

After the service, Rosa told Michael she wanted to go home. She did not want to attend the reception in the church hall. As they made their way to the door, Garrett Ferrell appeared in front of them. "Please, Mrs. Charpelli, can't you stay for just a few minutes? There are so many people here who would like to extend their condolences. It would mean a lot to them if you stayed."

"I suppose I could, but not for long. I am tired, very tired."

An hour later, the limousine pulled up in front of their house. Rosa looked out of the car window at the massive brick house in front of them. "I hate this place, Michael. I cannot wait to leave it. It was never home to me," Rosa said.

Michael opened the door and Rosa stepped into the hallway. She let out a gasp. The inside of the house was in complete devastation. Every piece of furniture in the entry had been torn apart. Dirt from the tall planters in the hallway was strewn across the floor. Cushions from the chairs had been slashed open.

Rosa screamed and backed out the door. "Look at this place. We've been robbed! Call 911, Michael. Don't go in the house."

When the police arrived they searched the house and found no one in it. The entire house was in shambles. Every room had been destroyed and torn to pieces.

"Everything is such a mess, I really can't tell you if anything has been taken without your help," the officer said. "Did you keep jewelry or cash in the house? How about fire arms?"

"No guns and very little jewelry," Michael answered. "There's a wall safe in the upstairs bathroom. That was my father's idea. You can check to see if it is empty. Jesus, I can't believed someone robbed us on the day we buried my dad."

The officer reported back, saying that it looked like the contents of the safe had been thrown on the floor. "Seems to me that whoever did this was looking for something in particular. Do you have any idea, Mrs. Charpelli?"

"No. I just want to leave here right now. Michael, please take me to a hotel. I don't want to stay here," Rosa said nervously.

"We'll have a full investigation. The department will send someone out to check for fingerprints. Mrs. Charpelli. Do you have an alarm system?" the officer asked.

"Yes. I don't know why it didn't go off. I set it right before we left the house. Frank always told me to set the alarm." She began to cry and Michael led her out of the house. He arranged for them to stay at a hotel.

After three days the police had finished their investigation. They reported to Michael that no fingerprints or footprints were found in the house. As far as they could ascertain nothing was taken. It appeared that who ever broke into the house was looking for something in particular. Before Rosa returned to gather her personal belongings Michael had made sure that the house was put back in order. It was a difficult task. Most everything had to be removed since it was either torn apart or broken. When he opened the door for his mother to enter, she hesitated. Walking slowly up the stairs, Rosa could hardly bring herself to go into the bedroom. There wasn't much there. Michael had the bed made and a new nightstand put next to it in case his mother decided to stay for the night.

She sat down on the bed and picked up the framed picture of she and Frank. It was the last one taken of them together just a few months past. She wiped her hand across it being careful not to cut herself on the shattered glass. Michael had found it on the floor. "Why, Frank? Why has someone done this to us? First you are taken from me and now all my memories are broken," Rosa said out loud.

"Mom, who are you talking to?" Michael asked sticking his head in the door.

"I am talking to your father. I talk to him all the time. Michael, come sit by me. I have something I want to tell you." Michael sat down and took his mother's hand.

"There is a convent in Rome called Casa Santo Teresa. It is the original home to the Sisters of Mercy. When I was a child and got sick with the polio my parents sent me there to live. They thought the prayers of the sisters would cure me. It was nice there. I remember the gardens. Each time I have gone there to visit it has given me a sense of peace. I have decided I want to go there to live out the rest of my life. Father Bridle said that the Sister's of Mercy could arrange for me to stay there."

"But, Mom…"

"Let me finish, Michael," Rosa said, putting her fingers to his lips. "I can work in the gardens and pray. I hear voices in my head that tell me I should go. My heart will always be sad, but I will heal there. I know I will never want to live in this house again. There are just too many bad memories. You, my dear son, need to finish school and make a life for yourself."

Michael was quiet for a moment, realizing that it would probably be best for her right now. If he tried to change her mind, she might stay just for him. She was a young woman, only in her fifties, but the last week had changed her completely. Perhaps after a few years there, she would come back to the states to live. "I'll miss you terribly, Mom. I'll come visit you as soon as school is over." He put his arms around her and held her close. Yes, he was going to miss her, just like he missed his father.

"Will you be upset if I am not here for your graduation?" she asked. "I need to go soon. I just want to get it over with. Without your father in the audience, I don't think it will be the same. He would have been so proud. He probably would have stood up and clapped. He was really looking forward to coming to your graduation." Michael choked back his tears. This was the worst time in his whole life.

Even the smallest mosquito could become an annoyance to Jakuta. He had become accustomed to the sweltering heat of the day and the cold nights, but the insects were a constant irritation to his skin. Flapping his ears to keep them away, Jakuta could feel the prick of their stingers as they pierced his thick hide. Throwing a trunk full of dust over his back he would have relief for a few minutes. It was a never-ending cycle.

Chapter Fifteen

"I want those papers! Do you hear me? I want them now and I want to know where in the hell my money is. Twenty-seven million fucking dollars. Where is it? That little bastard took the money out of the account that was set up in his name. How did he find it?" Garrett slammed his fist down on his desk. "You stupid bastard, you couldn't even make the break-in look like a robbery. How stupid are you? Why didn't you get those papers from him before you took care of him?"

"I just assumed they would be in his coat pocket," Ari replied in a whining voice. "We asked him over and over, but he refused to talk. He knew too much so even without the papers we had to carry out the plan."

"Without the papers! I'm sure I could have persuaded him to give them to me. Why didn't you come and get me? Ari Goldman, you are becoming less and less useful to me everyday. You find those papers and you bring them to me. Do you understand?"

"Yes, Mr. Ferrell. I'll find them, don't worry."

"I don't have to worry, Ari. You do. I have to leave for Frank's memorial service. My son is waiting for me. I suggest you take this time to look again for those documents." Garrett pushed Ari out of the way as he headed out the door. "Wait in the bathroom until I leave. I don't want anyone to see you," Garrett growled at him.

He greeted his son in the outer office with a smile on his face. "Good to see you, Elliott. I still can't understand why it took Michael so long to set up this memorial service. Since his mother is in Rome I thought he would just forgo it."

"He's having a tough time. He's studying for finals and still trying to get over his father's death. This is the best he could do." Elliott replied.

Carol Grey picked up her hat and gloves. She was dreading the memorial service but there was no way she could get out of attending it. She was startled when Ari came into her office.

"Did Charpelli give you something to keep for him before he died?" he asked, abruptly.

"What is it you're looking for?" She tried to sound convincing.

Ari moved toward her and grabbed her arm, pulling it behind her back, he asked again, "I said…did Frank give you something to hold for him?"

"Let go of me! You're hurting my arm. No! Frank never gave me anything," she moaned.

Ari released his grip. "You better be telling me the truth."

Carol held her arm, grimacing in pain. "I have no idea what you're talking about. Leave me alone." She grabbed her purse and rushed past him.

The next morning when she arrived at work Carol went directly to Garrett's office. She passed by his receptionist without stopping and burst into his office.

Garrett was startled by her sudden appearance in front of him. "What do you want, Carol? Did we have an appointment?"

"Why, why did you do it? You didn't need to kill Frank. He was a good man. You are an evil bastard, Garrett Ferrell."

"I shall take that as a compliment. You know why Frank had to be eliminated, Carol. It was for the good of the company. Once you are in, you are in all the way and there is no room for anyone who will not follow the rules."

"What about the others on this floor, are they next in line? Am I on your list?"

"I do believe they know their place. A little mishap like what happened to Frank reinforces their loyalty to me. Besides, I pay them well. For enough money they will jump through hoops for me. It's unfortunate that every once in a while someone comes along that wants to be a hero."

"Mr. Ferrell…please, let me go. I will walk out that door right now and you will never see me again. Nothing that was ever said or done in this office will go with me. Please." She began to sob and fell to her knees in front of his desk. "I can't do this anymore."

"Get up, Carol, you're making an ass of yourself. Sit down in the chair." He reached across the desk and pushed a box of tissues in front of her.

"I am a prisoner. Everything I do is monitored and you have someone sitting in front of my house every night. I cannot even sleep in peace. Let me leave this place," Carol pleaded.

"I am certainly not stopping you from leaving," Garrett said.

"I don't believe that, Mr. Ferrell. I have been threatened by your men before and I know if I leave without your consent I will be at their mercy."

"This is all a complete fabrication, Carol. I have no idea what you are talking about." He pondered for a moment. "I may consider letting you resign, but I have a few more tasks that need to be taken care of and the sooner the better. You are to create a new investment company for me, set it up completely and then transfer about ten million from one of the obscure banks in South America. Secondly, I want you to help me find out how Frank found out about the money in the overseas account. Someone had to tell him. When I find that person they are going to die. If you can take care of those two things, we will talk again at the end of the week about your dismissal." Garrett smiled.

"Now, Carol, don't you worry about a thing. I will make sure you are taken care of." She cringed. She was well aware of what those words meant.

Carol slowly rose from the chair and left the office. Garrett picked up the telephone, "Yes, the building is beginning to crumble. The threats to close her down are no longer working. I will get back to you."

Garrett walked over to the sideboard and poured himself a glass of brandy. He needed something to steady his nerves. Carol Grey was his one big mistake. He should have done away with her years ago, but he needed her in his operation. He was surprised at the wealth of knowledge she possessed about the business. It had been necessary to make her believe that she would go to prison for a long time if she didn't cooperate with him. Along with his threats against her life and her mother's he had kept her under his thumb for a long time, but now he may have to make other plans for her.

ꕥ ꕥ ꕥ ꕥ

The papers were still missing a month after Frank died and Garrett still refused to let Carol leave the company. His constant threats kept her paralyzed. She now feared for her life.

Garrett knew that Frank was a shrewd man. He wouldn't have discarded the papers. Someone had them and he would find them. He knew that Rosa was out of the picture. She was not allowed to bring anything into the convent with her except her rosary, family pictures and her bible. Everything else would be provided for her. Garrett made sure that her small satchel was thoroughly checked at the airport by one of his employees and the bible was thoroughly searched. Even the frames on the family pictures were removed. She did not have the papers. There were only a few other likely suspects: Carol, Ari and Michael. It wouldn't be too hard to reel Michael in. Garrett picked up the phone and dialed Elliott's number. "I have a proposition for you, Elliott. I know you are not anxious to go to work but I am going to reorganize some of the positions in this office. You and Michael could run it together. I think it would be a fitting tribute to his father and give him a chance to make some money. It would deal mostly with overseas trading with a few of the Middle East countries. Are you interested?"

"Well, why start at the bottom when you can start at the top? Is it eight to five, five days a week or am I going to spend every waking hour at the office like you do?"

"It depends on how diligent you are," Garrett answered.

"It would be nice to work with Michael. Let me pass it by him and I'll let you know."

"Well, how kind of you to say you'll get back to me. I'm offering you a position that most men would kill for and you'll get back to me? I'll give you forty-eight hours and then you are on your own. I thought that this might be an opportunity for Michael to get started on a good level."

Elliott laughed. "You don't know much about Michael. He is a real go-getter. I have no doubt that he'll succeed in anything he takes on."

That remark peaked Garrett's interest. "Is he like his father? Is it all about money?"

"Not at all. Michael is real laid back until you offer him a challenge. We have been pushing each other to the edge for the last four years. Tell him he can't do something and I guarantee you he will prove you wrong. I'll call him tonight and see what he says."

Garrett had to keep Michael under scrutiny. Having him in the company would keep him close by. With all of the people he had disposed of, he had never encountered a situation that he couldn't rectify. Garrett was seething inside. It was like an open sore that would not heal. He would not give up until he was sure those papers were destroyed and he had recouped his money. Within a few hours, Garrett had taken care of the loose ends that would make Michael's decision to say no to his offer very difficult. He had made sure that Michael Chapelli was now without funds.

§ § § §

Elliott tried to reach Michael several times that evening. He wasn't answering his phone. Elliott decided to ride out to his house. Michael's car was in the driveway. Elliott knocked several times before he tried the knob. The door was open.

"Hey Meatball, where are you?" Elliott called out. He took the steps to the second floor two at a time. A light shone under the door to Michael's room. Elliott rapped on the door, "You in there, Meatball?" No answer. He opened the door.

Michael was laying on the bed. He held up a bottle of Jack Daniels. "You see this bottle? The next time you see it, it will be empty. I plan on getting very drunk tonight. I will feel like crap in the morning, but its either get drunk or jump off the roof of this building."

"Feeling sorry for yourself tonight?" Elliott asked. "It's probably because you need to move out of this place. Why not come home and stay with me?"

"Well, I won't have to worry about this house much longer. You want to know how my day went? Go on, ask me how my day went?" He took a long drink from the bottle. "I found out the life insurance policy my father had was invalid since he committed suicide. Strike number one. Then when I went to the safe deposit box to retrieve all the jewelry my dad had bought over the years, it was gone and there are no records of any kind of savings accounts in my father's name. Strike two. So I went to the bank to see about unloading this house and I find out that my father had a second mortgage on this place. Why and what for, I have no idea. All I know is that I may owe money when the house is sold. Strike three and you're. So going to L.A. and opening my own marketing firm is out of the question. I guess that would be strike four. None of this makes sense. Where has the money gone and why a second mortgage on the house?"

"It may not be as bad as you think. My father has made us an offer. He wants you and I to come work for him. Not in the mailroom, but in the corporate office. We'll start at the top and work our way down."

The alcohol was beginning to take effect. "Why would he do that? That is plain stupid. He knows that I have no experience in international finance," he said, slurring his words. "Besides, I have no desire to work for your father. One Charpelli was enough."

"What do you mean by that?"

"Nothing. Not a damn thing. Tell him, thanks, but no thanks. I'll talk to you later. Close the door on your way out." Michael turned over and pulled the pillow over his head.

"I should have known you were not up to it," Elliott said.

Michael did not take his challenge. This time he had no desire to win or get even.

Yemaya stood over her newborn calf. She watched as he struggled to stand and then fell over again. He was too weak to continue on the journey to the water that was still miles away. The rest of the females hovered around her, watching as she prodded him with her trunk. They were tired and thirsty but it was their duty to stay with the matriarch of the herd. Standing a few hundred yards away was a pack of hungry hyenas. They would wait patiently until the calf died and the herd moved on. It may be a few days, but they would wait. They had nowhere else to go.

Yemaya tried once again to raise him, but she knew it was useless. His shallow breathing and glassy eyes were signs that he was not going to live. Yemaya had only three successful births in her life, yet she never gave up until she was sure there was not even one breath of life left in them. The herd was getting restless as the sun beat down on their backs.

Yemaya stepped back, the signal that the calf had died. Picking him up with her trunk she moved into the shade of a few barren acacia trees, giving herself time to mourn. It was then that the hyenas made their move. Slowly...stealthily...they moved closer. Yemaya sensed their presence and moved from under the tree. Laying the lifeless form on the ground, she reared her head and with one fell swoop of her trunk she picked up one on the hyenas and tossed him into the air. He let out a yelp as he hit the ground. Now he lay dead along with her calf. Unlike the elephants that would mourn the death of their young, the hyenas would eat one of their own.

Chapter Sixteen

It took only three weeks for the house to sell. Michael left the attorney's office with a check for twenty thousand dollars. After paying off the first and second mortgages on the house he was lucky that there was still a small profit. He planned on going home that afternoon and finish packing the rest of his things. Michael had two weeks to vacate the house. He was ready to get out of New York. Stopping by Starbucks, he got a large coffee to go and then headed downtown to Ferrell Enterprises. He wanted to pick up the rest of his father's things. Carol had called him several times to remind him that his father's personal effects were still in his office. She emphasized that there may be things he would want to keep.

He nodded to a few employees he knew and took the elevator to the nineteenth floor. Carol was still posted in the outer office, which was a surprise to Michael. He wondered what she was doing now that she no longer had anyone to work under.

"Hello, Miss Grey, I came to get the rest of my father's things. Do you mind if I go into his office?"

"No, by all means go on in." She let out a sigh of relief. Michael had *finally* come to the office. She opened the door and stepped back. It seemed so sterile now. All that remained of his father's presence was a neat stack of books on the desk and a rolled up map. Michael walked past the desk and opened the door to the bathroom. He looked up at the bar that ran across the window. The bar that had held the necktie that had taken the life out of his father. Michael slammed the door and walked back to the desk and sat down. He had no idea why he had even bothered, but he knew that the map his father had hung on the wall of the office was very important to him. He brought it with him from Italy.

"I'm so sorry about your father," Carol said. "He was a very nice man." She laid her hands on the book lying next to the map. Once again she had to find a way to communicate without anyone being aware of what she was doing. Her fingers tapped on it. Her eyes darted back and forth, from Michael to the book as she slowly pushed it in front of him. "I know this was one of his favorite books." She pushed it closer to him. "Here please take it with you."

He could sense that she was trying to tell him something. The book was on practical applications in accounting. Surely not one of his father's favorites. There was a piece of paper sticking out from between two pages. He casually opened the book. Written in the margin of the page were the words: *I need to see you in private soon. It is very important. Please say nothing. We are both being watched and followed everywhere we go. Just act natural. Please, please help me. You are my last hope.*

Michael looked up at Carol and she nodded slightly. "Do you want to take these things with you?" she asked.

"Yes. Thanks for everything, Miss Grey." He put his arm lightly around her in a formal hug.

"Six p.m. Brook Street Car Wash," she quickly whispered to him.

"Well, I'd better go. I have some more packing to do," Michael said. He was very confused.

"Goodbye Mr. Charpelli," she said, with pleading eyes.

In the elevator Michael wondered what was going on. He had never had any contact with Carol. His father mentioned her occasionally, but not with a large degree of fondness. Why was Carol being so secretive? Who was watching him? It seemed so urgent to her and it made him curious.

Getting into his car, Michael looked into the rear view mirror. He had no idea why, except that Carol had put that thought into his head that he was being followed. He saw nothing unusual until he was about halfway down the block. The black car parked two spaces behind him pulled out slowly and dropped in line behind him. The windshield of the car was tinted. Michael could not make out who was driving. Changing lanes several times, which was no easy task in downtown New York at four in the afternoon, Michael realized that the sedan was still several car lengths behind him. He picked up his cell phone and dialed. "Chris, hi, it's Michael Charpelli. I am right near your apartment building. Thought I might stop in for a few minutes. That okay with you?"

"Yeah, sure, Michael, come on by."

Chris was a classmate of Michael's at Princeton. He lived just a few miles away in a downtown high rise. Michael kept his eye on the black car. Pulling over in front of a liquor store he went inside to buy a bottle of wine. The car came to a stop across the street, but the driver did not get out. Michael now knew for sure that he was being followed. When he reached the apartment building he parked in the visitors section of the garage and got out just as the automobile passed by him. Michael stepped into the shadows behind a support pillar and waited. A few minutes later the car slowly descended the ramp and pulled out on to the street.

Michael was uneasy, but he managed to make his visit with Chris last for two hours. They talked about his father's death and his decision to leave New York. He tried to follow the conversation, but he could not get the remarks that Carol had made out of his mind.

Leaving work at her usual time, Carol Grey kept her routine the same as it had been for the last few years. She stopped by a neighborhood market and picked up a few things for dinner. Since her mother had died she ate very little, but today in particular Carol wanted her captors to think that every thing was as usual. Parking her car in front of her Brownstone, she carried her packages inside and made herself a bowl of soup. Carol looked at her watch. It was five o'clock. She had one hour. She ate her soup slowly. She washed the bowl and spoon and put them away in the cupboard.

Upstairs, she packed a small bag of clothing. She slipped into a jacket and put her passport and a stack of money into her jacket pocket. Carol checked once more to make sure she had everything and then walked past the window. The car was there in its usual spot. Leaving the light on, Carol closed her bedroom door and walked down the stairs. She picked up the kitchen telephone and dialed 911. When the operator answered, she screamed into the telephone, "Help me, there are two men in my house. 877 Field Street. Oh, God, here they come, they have guns!" She let the telephone drop to the floor as the operator continued to talk and then she waited. Carol stood by her back door, until she heard the sirens coming up the street. It sounded like at least two patrol cars. When they were within a block of the house, she opened the back door and ran across the yard. There seemed to be a lot of confusion going on in the front of the house. It was exactly what Carol had hoped for.

Seven blocks away from Carol's house, Michael pulled up in front of the car wash promptly at 6 o'clock. There was no sign of Carol. He waited for a few minutes and then went inside. The attendant handed him a ticket. "Just a wash or do you want a wax too?" the attendant asked.

"Actually, I am waiting for someone. A lady. She was supposed to meet me here," Michael said, looking around.

"Only one woman here right now and I think she's in the restroom," the man said.

"Well, give me a ticket. I'll have my car washed." He walked outside and just as he got back into his car, Carol motioned to him from the rear of the building. He pulled the car up onto the ramps and she quickly ran around to the passenger's side and got into the back seat just as the first blast of hot water and soap hit the car.

"Okay, I've had all the James Bond I need for one night. What is this all about and why was I being followed?

"I will tell you everything when we get to your house," she said.

"My house! Why my house and do you have to lay in the back seat?" Michael asked.

"When you get to your house pull into the garage. I'm sure they will be waiting for you to get home. Let me get inside before you turn on the lights." Another comment that baffled him.

When he arrived home, he noticed the same car that had followed him earlier in the day parked at the end of the street. Carol was right about one thing, he was being watched. After the garage door closed, Michael unlocked the kitchen door. Carol handed him her bag and she crawled out of the car, up the steps and into the kitchen. Sitting down, her back leaning against one of the cabinets, she was out of breath. When Michael turned on the light, Carol put her finger to her lips, giving him the signal not to talk to her. Michael pulled a piece of paper and a pen from the counter and dropped it next to her.

She wrote: *The house may be wired. We need to make sure before we talk that they are not listening. Open the patio door and I will meet you in the pool house.*

Michael was beginning to worry about her sanity. What was wrong with this woman? He watched her as she crawled across the floor and out the patio door. He fixed himself a drink and went out to the pool house. He had no idea what he was looking for, but he checked around the small enclosures for microphones and cameras the best he could.

"I guess we're safe for a little while. When they find out I am gone, they are going to start looking for me," Carol said.

"Who are they?" Michael growled. "Who in the hell are you talking about? This is one of the strangest situations I have ever been in. What's going on?"

"Where do you want me to start?" Carol asked.

"Might as well start at the beginning so I can make some sense out of this crap."

Carol let out a sigh and began talking. " I was raised by my mother. She made sure that I excelled in school. I was one of the smart kids that graduated from college at the age of twenty-one with a degree in computer science. I have always had a better than average memory when it comes to numbers. Ferrell was my first job after graduation."

"So, when I said start at the beginning I didn't mean you had to go back that far. Is all this information really necessary, Miss Grey?" Michael commented.

"I need to tell you this, Michael. I want you to truly understand how this mess all came about," she answered. She began again." Houston was Garrett's father. When I started working at Ferrell Enterprises, Houston was my boss.

"My first position was in the research department. Garrett was in charge of that department at that time, but it was a common joke that he did nothing but research the women in the department. My job was to investigate the companies that Ferrell was thinking about doing business with and make sure the companies were solvent. I found a big mistake with one of the companies just weeks after I started working there. Houston Ferrell came down from the third floor and congratulated me personally. I remember that day quite well because Houston made the comment that his son should have been more on the ball and found the mistake.

"Houston rewarded me by giving me the position of Mr. Gayle's assistant and it was a great honor. I got a large salary increase and I was thrilled not having to work with Garrett anymore.

"Daniel Gayle was the number one man in charge of the whole accounting department. He was a nice man…a very nice man. He was kind of bookish, not much to look at, but a soft and kind man. I loved my job. We had a great staff. Everyone was friendly and got along well. Of course the company was much smaller then. We had an office on Bank Street. It was only three stories high. Nothing at all like the new building."

The sound of a barking dog startled Carol. Afraid that someone might be lurking about outside she slid off of her chair and sat on the floor."

"After five years at my job, Houston Ferrell died in an explosion in his home. Garrett was given the power of attorney and appointed himself president of Ferrell Enterprises. It was quite a surprise to everyone since Houston had commented several times that his son was not interested in anything but money and didn't seem to grasp on to the concept of what the business was all about or even care. He was planning on naming someone else to the position when he retired. The speculation in the office is that Daniel would be given the job as company CEO, but since Garrett was Houston's only heir he took over. Cynthia stayed in Europe most of the time until her death from complications of pneumonia a few years later.

"When Garrett took over he hired almost a completely new staff and let all of the men on the third floor go except Daniel. There were ten new employees. Where he got them, I don't know, but he had each of them in his pocket. He lured them into the company with money. Lots of money. One of the men he hired was Ari Goldman. Ari was a smart man, but his appetite for wealth overshadowed his judgment many times. Ari was one of my least favorite people. He was a schemer and as money hungry as Garrett. I know now that he always had to have one employee working for him that was honest, like,

Daniel and your father. There had to be someone to take the fall if something happened."

Michael interrupted her. "I need another drink? Do you want one?"

"Yes, but hurry back."

When Michael returned Carol took a large swallow from the glass and resumed her story.

"So Garrett had a sophisticated computer system set up that kept track of everything that was going on. The rumor in the office was that Garrett was doing undercover work for the CIA. I thought that was preposterous, but he never denied it and in some way it made the employees feel important.

"Right after Garrett took over the company, he and his wife began to spend money at an alarming rate. He bought the mansion on Long Island, several cars, and an eighty-foot yacht. His wife shopped on a daily basis buying jewelry and furs. They took extravagant trips and gave lavish parties for their friends.

"When Daniel tried to warn him that they were spending too much money, Garrett would scream at him and tell him to find more. He had a very bad temper. That was also the time that he moved the whole company to the new building." Carol stopped talking. It was if she was coming to a part in her story that was difficult for her.

"And then everything in the company began to change. Michael do you know there are organizations and syndicates all over the world looking for large, individually owned companies that are in financial difficulty? They watch to see how the businesses are doing and when the signs show up that the company is in trouble, they move in. At first they move slow spinning their web of deception. They find out everything they can about the people in charge. Mostly trying to figure out how money hungry they are and how moral they are. Those two things are what they are looking for. When they find someone like Garrett, they rub their hands together. He was wined and dined by the best of them. He and his wife received lavish gifts from these people along with empty promises. Knowing that wild game hunting was his thing, they took Garrett on expensive safaris and then they reeled him in like a fish in bowl. They said if he would agree to let them put money in his company for just a short time, they could give him a large fee. He knew his corporation was in trouble, so he took the bait. Within months, large sums of money were coming in and out of the company at an alarming rate from places we had never dealt with before. They were from shell corporations that had been set up as legal businesses but had no assets. Most of the money was from large drug cartels in South America and arms dealers in the Middle East or others trying to avoid paying large tax bills. Garrett's explanation to us was that the company was now involved in international trading. It was crazy. We were now all sworn to secrecy. No one on the floor could tell anyone else what was going on with his accounts.

"I should have quit then. I guess I wasn't much better than the rest of those who were kept on staff. The money was good and it made it easier to overlook things going on around you." She stopped for a moment. "Besides I didn't want to give up my job working with Daniel." A flicker of light from a passing car stopped Carol's story. She jumped up and looked out the small cabana window. The car was already gone. She continued on.

"Garrett also took on another hobby. He joined the Twelve Elephant Club and began taking regular hunting trips to Africa. It is a very exclusive club and it cost him a million dollars just to become a member."

"Why is this important?" Michael asked, remembering the safari he went on with Garrett.

"Because he couldn't get enough of it. It was like a sickness. It was eerie. He always wanted to tell you the story of how he killed each one of the poor beasts. He even joked one time about hunting humans and wondered what that would be like. He spent huge sums of money on hunting rifles and safaris to Africa."

Carol hesitated for a moment. "I'm getting off track. It's all so crazy." She began again.

"It was around that time that Garrett began to realize that I was valuable to him. He knew I had more knowledge about his father's business than him. You see, Michael, I was handpicked, just like your father and the others. He made sure I had a good salary and lots of perks. He wanted to keep me happy. He made one mistake. He did not realize that Daniel Gayle and I were a formidable team.

"With all the money going out, and not much coming in, Daniel and I spent long hours together pouring over the accounts, trying to find ways to generate more business. We were more concerned about all of the employees than we were about Garrett. We were afraid they would all be left with nothing when the business went under. Those longs hours we spent together brought Daniel and I much closer." Carol hesitated a moment. This wasn't a part of the story she relished telling Michael. "When we first began our affair I felt so guilty. Daniel was a married man. As much as we tried to stay away from each other we couldn't. We were deeply in love with each other. He had children and he was afraid if Garrett found out he would fire us both. We both knew that even though Garrett professed that he was a devout Catholic and would never divorce his wife he had many women outside of his marriage. So we continued on, hoping we could find a way to someday be together all of the time."

Michael interjected his thoughts. "I guess that was about the time that Elliott told me that his parents were always fighting."

"When Garrett found out that we were seeing each other, he brought us into his office. He condemned us for our actions and said we were both destined for hell. And then he said that we owed him our lives and sent us back to work. It didn't take long to figure out that remark. He said that he expected us to conform to the new business ventures he would be involved in. I knew it was more of a threat than a suggestion.

"Daniel was the first to realize how deeply the company was involved in illegal activity. When he went to Garrett with his suspicions, Garrett wanted to give him a huge raise. Daniel said no. He decided it wasn't worth taking the risk and decided it was better if he left the company. I decided to leave, too. So Daniel and I both wrote letters of resignation and sent them to Garrett.

"Garrett called us both into his office. He was seething with anger. He threw a glass vase against the wall and it shattered sending glass flying everywhere. He took both of our letters and ripped them into shreds. Garrett said he would tell Daniel's wife and children about our affair. He also said he could prove that we had been skimming money from the company. I was stunned. I knew then that he wasn't rational anymore."

Michael interrupted, "Did Daniel quit?"

"No. He wanted time to come up with another plan, but he was feeling uneasy after facing Garrett. He told me that he was being followed and that he was afraid that Garrett was having his every move monitored. I knew that I was being monitored, too. Garrett seemed to know my every move. We decided to let things cool off a bit and make a realistic plan. Garrett seemed to settle down and we were off the hook for a while.

"Two weeks later, Daniel was run off of the road on his way home from work. His car rolled down an embankment and caught fire. He died in the wreck.

"I was devastated by Daniel's death. At the funeral Garrett took me aside and said he was so sorry about what had happened, but it could happen to anyone that doesn't follow orders. I couldn't believe what I was hearing. I knew then that my life was now in his hands. What could I do at that point? My mother was an invalid. I could never run away and leave her and I knew that Garrett was not going to let me out of his sight.

"I grieved over Daniel and tried to concentrate on the rigorous training that Garrett and Ari Goldman began putting me through. I was told what to say and when to say it. I was going to be the liaison between them and the new man who was going to take Daniel's place. In other words, I was their new spy.

"You see Garrett had already put Ari in his pocket. Ari was an easy mark. He was money hungry and owed a huge gambling debt to some unsavory people. He also had a wife like Garretts' who enjoyed spending money. With all of his money worries gone, Ari was willing to do anything that Garrett asked of him, even commit murder.

"I met him a couple times. I never really liked him." Michael said. "Are you telling me that Ari was a murderer?"

"Wait, Michael. Let me go on and you will get the whole picture."

"You see by this time Garrett was way over his head with his new company business. His greed was overwhelming, but neither Garrett nor Ari were smart enough to run the enormous amount of business that was generating millions of dollars for the company. They had to pick on another innocent soul. Once again they needed a middleman who knew how to run a company. The new man's name was Ralph Jillion.

"I wanted to tell him to run, to get away from the company as fast as he could, but Ralph had his own agenda. He wanted to make a lot of money even if he had to look the other way once in a while. He told me that is what you have to do when you're involved in big business. I knew I couldn't count on him to be my ally.

"By now, more money was coming in than Garrett could clean up. So he opened accounts in his employee's names all over the world. Accounts that his employees had no idea existed. He put huge sums of money in their accounts. They were so spread out; no one would ever know to look for them. That is, except Garrett and I. There were statements issued each year to the employees with their actual retirement account fund. None of them knew that on paper they were all millionaires. All of this was my job.

"It took Ralph over three years to really catch on to what was really going on and how illegal it all was. He made a mistake of going to Garrett and telling him he wanted a bigger piece of the pie. What a foolish man. He threatened Garrett. A big mistake."

"Please tell me he resigned," Michael interjected.

Carol shook her head. "I wish I could. It was on a Friday afternoon and Ralph had told me that he wasn't feeling well. He had been suffering all week with indigestion and seemed nervous and unsteady on his feet. That day, he said he was nauseated and had a bad headache. Around four o' clock, he called me into his office. He was holding his chest and gasping. Just as I picked up the phone to call 911, Ari came running in. He put Ralph on the floor and grabbed the phone from my hand. I remember hearing him telling the emergency operator that Ralph was having a heart attack. We waited five, and then ten minutes and they didn't come. Ari was giving him mouth-to-mouth resuscitation, but I could see that Ralph was slipping away. I couldn't believe it was taking that long. I wanted to pick him up and take him to the hospital, but Ari said that would be too dangerous. I went back out to my office and called 911 again. I screamed at them and asked what was taking so long. They said they had no report of anyone calling, but they would come right away. I remember standing there with the telephone in my hand, knowing that Ari really didn't call 911. He must have held down the disconnect button while he pretended to call. He really wasn't giving him CPR. Ralph was dead by the time the ambulance arrived. Was it murder? Yes, but who could prove it? Garrett was standing in the hallway when the ambulance came. Once again he put on a great act. I was so sick to my stomach I thought I had to tell someone.

"Garrett and Ari were so calculating. They anticipated my every move. That evening when I entered the church and made my way down the aisle to the confessional, someone came up behind me and grabbed my arm. I couldn't see his face. He just kept pushing me down the aisle. He whispered to me that if I loved my mother, I better watch what I confessed. I found out later that his name was Howard. He was the new enforcer that was part of Garrett's staff.

"My life became a living hell. I was just too good at my job and Garrett needed me. I worried constantly about what was going to happen next. I never had a time when I thought I could go to the authorities without them getting to my mother or me first. At first when she became ill, I thought that they had done something to her, but the doctors confirmed that her kidneys and liver were failing. When she died, they all came to her funeral. I felt like it was a ritual being held by the devil himself."

"Wait just a minute, Carol. You mean with all of this going on there wasn't one person in that whole damn organization that you could trust—someone who could help you."

"There were a few I thought I might be able to talk to but things changed so rapidly. People would come and go without even a notice. They would be there on Friday and Monday morning they were gone. I was told they quit, or got transferred. Sometimes no one would know what happened to them."

Michael sat up straight. "And no one asked questions? Do you think Garrett was doing away with people even then?"

"I don't know. And then for a while, everything changed. Garrett promoted your father and all of the large overseas accounts seemed to disappear. We were back to doing what the company was built on— the honest handling of financial investments. I don't know if Garrett got scared or had enough or what caused the change, but I tried to convince myself that maybe Daniel's death was really an accident and that Ari did call the emergency number for Ralph. They began being nice to me and I thought that maybe all the things they had said to me were just empty threats, even though I knew I could never leave the company until they were ready to let me go. And now I want to tell you about your father."

Michael got up from the lawn chair. "I don't know if I really want to hear the next part, Carol."

"You have to Michael and when I'm finished if you want to strangle me right here and dump my body in the river, I will not blame you.

"I know you won't believe this, but your father was awed with money, Michael. It wasn't in a bad way. He believed that hard work gave you good results. He even kept notes about money. He had lists of things he wanted to buy and places he wanted to visit. He wasn't greedy, Michael. Most of his money was earmarked for you and your mother. I can't tell you how many times I tried to warn him, but he loved Ferrell Enterprises and I knew he wouldn't believe me. Garrett had tightened his security on me so I had to be careful about everything I said. I knew I couldn't help your father get out of the mess until I got the last piece of the puzzle—the code to get into

Garrett's computer. I also knew that Garrett was beginning to get irritated with your father. I dropped subtle hints hoping somehow your father would catch on. He didn't, but he knew something was not right and so when he went to Garrett and gave his resignation, Garrett gave him a huge bonus. He took it. Something happens to people when a huge sum of money enters into the equation. I trusted your father. I took the chance and was able to get through to him about the situation. I know you don't believe me, but I honestly wanted to save him."

She began to cry. "You have to believe me, Michael. I tried so hard to get him away from there. He would never give up his loyalty to Garrett Ferrell until he finally began to figure things out for himself. To make matters even worse your father was confiding in Ari Goldman. He is Garrett's right hand man. Your father must have told Ari that he had evidence to convict Garrett. I suppose your father never knew what Garrett was really capable of. And when I found him in the bathroom…"

Michael's hands tightened into fists. "He never committed suicide, did he? They killed him! The bastards killed him. That son of a bitch had him killed!"

"You're right, Michael, your father didn't take his own life, they killed him just like they killed the others and just like they are going to kill me. It was Ari and a man named Howard who did that terrible thing for Garrett. And now they are still looking for those incriminating papers that your father comprised and they are not going to give up until they find them. That is why Garrett had your house ransacked. They are scared, really scared this time. I wanted to tell you Michael, but I knew if I did, there would just be two more people added to their list of dispensable commodities—you and your mother, because Garrett thinks that one of you have the papers."

"God…I can't believe this. I want to go over there and kill that son of a bitch right now."

"And you would be charged with murder and there would still be no evidence of wrong doing by Ferrell Enterprises."

"He can't get away with this."

"He can and he will unless those papers are found. You see they are the only tangible evidence. Each day's transactions were taken out of the computer and legal ones put in. There were men working on our floor who were actually involved in the legal part of the business. Each day the hard drive from your father's computer was removed and destroyed. Garrett has the only computer with the names of all the people he is doing business with and some kind of code that will destroy the hard drive if anyone ever gets into his the office and tries to confiscate it. He thought he had a foolproof plan. He never thought I would get brave enough to give your father the information. There are some real heavy hitters on that list that your father made."

"But how did my father get into the master file? How did he find the code?"

"It was me, Michael. I was the one that was finally able to get the last piece of the puzzle. Garrett was logging onto his computer one day when I walked into his office. We got into a heated argument and he grabbed me by the arm and almost pulled me across the desk. And there it was. The code. I quickly memorized it and then wrote it down. It was just a simple seven-letter name… Morritt. I should have known it would have something to do with elephants. Charles Morritt was a magician from Yorkshire, England. He was the man that invented the trick of making an elephant disappear. He sold his secret to Houdini for a great deal of money. When Houdini realized how simple the trick really was he felt deceived. Garrett loved that story and I suppose he thought it was amusing to use a code connected with deceit. I have also seen the inside group use the code name Ironman when sending memos back and forth. The Ferrell company was built on Garrett's greed so all it needed was a little crack in it to make it crumble. I provided that crack when I finally was able to move just two accounts and then I gave it to your father."

Michael shook his head. "You! If it was you why didn't you take the information to the authorities instead of giving it to my dad?"

"Two reasons. I neither had the time or place where I could get out of their sight and secondly, I thought it would protect your father if Garrett knew he had that information. I was mistaken. Nothing can stand in the way of Garrett's wrath when he wants something. I am so sorry, Michael."

"On one hand I think you are a yellow coward and you stood by while innocent men died, on the other hand I can see that you would never have been able to prove it. It was your word against his. But there must have been someone out there that would believe you?" Michael said, angrily

"And who would that be at this point? If I had come to you, Michael, would you have believed me? After all, you and Elliott are friends. If I accused Elliot's father of money laundering would you have believed me? What would you have done, knowing that if you went to the authorities Garrett would prove that it was all your father's doing and that he had skimmed large sums of money from the company. Especially since he had an account he never knew existed with millions of dollars in it. Even if everything went right it was still an impossible situation."

"Dammit, I don't know…no, I probably would have tried to get my father away from there."

"Do you think he would have gone? By that time they would have told him that your life and your mother's life was in jeopardy. He loved you both, very much. The papers were the only leverage he had and now they are gone too." Carol wiped the tears from her eyes. "There is one more thing I wanted to tell you. Garrett set up accounts in his employee's names all over the world. One of those accounts was in your father's name. He put large sums of money into it every month. That was in case he had to prove that, like the others before him, your father was stealing money from the company. On Wednesday, I took the money out of the account and hid it in a local account. They will never find it."

"How much is in it?" Michael asked.

"Twenty-seven million," she replied.

"Twenty-seven million! Did I hear you right, did you say twenty-seven million?"

Carol nodded her head yes.

"I want that money. I am going to teach that bastard that two can play his dirty game. Somehow, somewhere I am going to get even with him—Oh, my God, Elliott—does he know anything about all of this?"

Carol shook her head. "Not that I know of, but it probably won't be long before Garrett gets him involved on one level or another. Garrett is a maniacal. I am sure he is capable of anything, including corrupting his son."

Michael began pacing back and forth across the small space. "So, was it Garrett who took out the second mortgage on this house, changed the insurance and took everything out of the safe deposit box?"

"I am sure he did. He wants to keep you close to him until he finds those papers. I suppose he thinks you have them."

"What's going to happen now, Miss Grey?" Michael asked.

"When they find they me, and they will; they will kill me," she said, almost matter of fact. "They are relentless, Michael. Garrett will never stop looking for me. I will have to be in hiding for the rest of my life."

"Well, I don't think so. We'll have to think up something to keep you safe. I should hate you, but I don't. I feel sorry for you and that may be even worse."

She burst into tears again, sobbing into her hands. "You don't hate me any worse than I hate myself."

"How much time do you think we have?" Michael asked.

"As soon as the police realized the 911 call tonight was a hoax, Garrett knew I was gone. I don't believe they will come after you right away. I am their main priority right now." She sighed. "You have no idea how long I have waited to tell someone what was going on. If I didn't think that your life was in jeopardy too, I would have never put this all on you."

Michael wasn't listening. He had to come up with a plan and quickly. "You'll have to stay here until I can figure this out. After it gets dark tonight, you can sneak back into the house. We'll just have to take our chances that they haven't planted any bugs in it. I'll check it out the best I can. Garrett Ferrell is going to be sorry for what he did. Real sorry. I am going to destroy him bit by bit."

"I can help you, Michael. I know everything about Garrett. I know all the passwords and names his associates use. You'll have to get rid of Ari and Howard in order to get to him."

"By the time we get through with Garrett Ferrell there will be quite a few people after him," Michael said.

"I want to give you one more warning, Michael. Do not trust anyone who tries to contact you or get information. At this point, no one is above suspicion. Take your time and don't make any rash decisions. It may cost you dearly. Can I ask you a question, Michael?

"What?"

"Have you ever been afraid of dying? I mean with all the crazy stunts you and Elliott pulled did you ever really think about dying?

Michael hesitated. “No, I don’t think I really gave it much thought.”

“Think about it now.”

Yemaya and her herd were on the move again across the Savannah. Occasionally the females would cross paths with another herd of elephants. There was always a cordial greeting of low grunts and slowly rubbing against each other. They were of one species.

A few hundred yards away a sea of black and white stripes followed each other to the next feeding ground. They kept their distance.

Passing an occasional thatch of grass the elephants would stay clear of the rhinos that had taken refuge there. Three or four rhinos watched as the elephants moved by. Their nostrils flared and they lowered their heads, keeping the lethal weapon molded to the front of their nose ready for any intrusion. They were not enemies, nor were they friends.

Miles away in an animal refuge compound a young female rhino slept with her back pressed against a male elephant calf, twice her size, but the same age. They stayed together out of necessity to combat the loneliness they felt from being abandoned by their mothers. During the day they played outside together— the elephant wrapping his trunk over the leathery hide of the rhino. For now, they were the best of friends, but as time passed and they grew strong, they would be placed in larger pens with their own kind. He would be an elephant and she would be a rhino. They would not be enemies, nor would they be friends.

Chapter Seventeen

With Carol safely inside the house and asleep in his parent's room, Michael finally gave into the exhaustion that filled his body. Entrenched in a deep sleep it took him a few moments to realize that someone was ringing the doorbell. He sat up in bed and looked at the clock. It was seven a.m. Putting on his pants, he hopped into the hall and quickly went downstairs.

He took a deep breath and opened the front door.

A middle-aged man, in a wrinkled, brown suit, stood leaning against the doorframe. "Yes, what is it?" Michael asked in an irritated voice, to show his disapproval of the early morning intrusion.

The man reached into his pocket and pulled out a small leather wallet, which he flipped open to reveal a shiny New York City Police Department Badge. "Sorry to wake you so early Mr. Charpelli, but I have a busy schedule today. My name is Detective Harold McCabe. I got a little mystery on my hands and I was wondering if I could ask you a few questions?"

"Come in," Michael said, showing him into the living room. "Let's sit in here."

"Well, it seems like Carol Grey has disappeared. She was your father's secretary. Do you remember her?"

"Of course I do. I just saw her on Wednesday when I went by to pick up my father's books. What do you mean disappeared?"

Detective McCabe reiterated the story about the 911 call to her house. "Carol Grey was not there when they arrived and no one has seen her since. We're not sure if someone took her out of the house by force or she left on her own volition. There was no evidence of a struggle. Either way, she's gone and we have no idea where she is. We're just touching base with everyone who saw her in the past week. Did she say anything about going away or did she seem nervous or worried about anything that you can recall?"

"Not at all. Carol had only one demeanor, very curt and stoic and she was the same on Wednesday when I saw her."

McCabe rubbed his chin. "Seems like that office is plagued with strange happenings. The last three people she had worked for have died and now she's gone." He positioned himself on the front of the chair. "No one ever knew for sure why Daniel Gayle's car went off the road. Wasn't raining that day. Just seemed sort of strange. And then Ralph Jillion had what they said was a heart attack and there was that mix-up on the emergency calls. Jillion was rushed off and cremated before anyone got to make sure if that was really what happened to him."

"What are you saying? Why are you telling me all of this?" Michael said, trying to sound convincing.

"I was called when they found your father. I checked out that bathroom and the way the chair was laying on its side. Even standing on that chair he wouldn't have been able to reach that window rod. Hell, I'm five inches taller than he was and I could barely reach it."

Michael could feel his throat tightening. "What are you saying? The investigators told me that he stood on the windowsill. Are you saying that someone killed my father?"

McCabe put his hands up. “No, just making observations. The team that investigated your father’s death said it was suicide—plain and simple. I’m not sure I really agree with them, but who am I to open a new can of worms. Just trying to tie up some loose ends.” He hesitated for a minute. “Sure seems strange to me.”

Michael stood up. “Look, Detective McCabe, my father was really depressed before it all happened. He had no enemies. I have no reason to believe it wasn’t his doing. I am just trying to get my life back together. I have sold this house and I am going to go to Rome to see my mother and then move to Los Angeles. I cannot and will not put my mother through any more grief. Until you have concrete evidence to prove your allegations, I suggest you leave me out of this. If I see or hear from Miss Grey before I leave I will let you know. Please close the door on your way out.”

“I’d appreciate that,” McCabe said. “Here’s my card. Keep it handy. Thanks for your time.”

Upstairs, with the door slightly ajar, Carol had been listening to the whole conversation. She met Michael at the door to the bedroom. “Good job, Michael. You are a quick learner.”

Later that morning at Ferrell Enterprises, Detective McCabe sat in front of Garrett Ferrell’s desk chewing on a toothpick. “So as I see it, Michael Charpelli seems on the level. He didn’t seem to want to get involved in an ongoing investigation. We’ve had him tailed for over two weeks now and he hasn’t talked to anyone other than your son and a friend of his.

His father's death was a real sore subject and he just wants to close the book on it."

Garrett narrowed his eyes. "Then where is Carol Grey? I want you to find her. I know she has those papers. I want you to find her and make sure she is never heard from again."

"It's not going to be as simple as you think. I have the airports and the bus stations covered. This is an easy city to get lost in," McCabe said.

Yemaya surveyed the smoldering expanse of grass that lay in front of her and the herd. It was up to her to find a way around it. Leading the group to the far edge of the brush fire, she and the others nervously traipsed across the steaming mud to safety.

Chapter Eighteen

It was up to Michael now. He had all the evidence he needed to start avenging his father's death and ease the state of grief his mother now lived in. He didn't care how long it would take. It was going to happen. Garrett Ferrell would be destroyed!

The first part of Michael's plan was fairly easy. Leaving Carol in his house, he took a taxi across town to the convent of the Sisters of Mercy. Stepping out of the cab, he took a deep breath. This was his last hope. If this part of his plan did not work he would have to go to the authorities with the papers. He wondered how many of the FBI employees were on Garrett's payroll.

He walked up the path leading to the stone building that housed the Sisters of Mercy and dropped the handle on the doorknocker.

"Oh, Michael, dear, I want to tell you once again how sorry I am about what happened to your father," Mother Superior, Mary Rose said. She put both her hands on Michael's cheeks. "You're mother has always been so dear to me. How is she doing? How awful for you."

"Can we take a walk in the garden?" he asked.

Walking down the path lined with red roses, Michael took a deep breath and began talking. "I have a very important question to ask you. If your answer is no, I will completely understand. You see, Sister, I have reason to believe that my father did not commit suicide, but was actually murdered." Sister Mary Rose let out a small gasp. "There is a woman that knows more about this matter than she should and her life is in danger. I need desperately to get her out of harm's way so that she can continue to help me prove what really happened. I want to take her to Rome to stay at the convent. I wanted to know if it would be possible to borrow a habit from one of your sisters to use as a disguise? I hope you believe me. It is all too complicated for me to explain to you, but I promise that I am telling you the truth."

"What evil person would do such a thing to a man like your father? I can do you one better, Michael. I have several nuns here that are ready to take their annual pilgrimage to Rome. They can accompany you and it will make for an even better disguise."

"Oh, I could never do that, Sister Mary Rose. I would never want to put anyone else in danger."

"Nonsense! No one would dare attack four nuns on a plane. I will personally ask the sister and we will all pray for your safe passage. It would relieve my heart to know that your father's soul is safe in heaven. Now give me a few minutes."

Sister Mary Rose was not a novice at helping people escape persecution. Many times she had helped hide away innocent citizens whose only sin was their choice of faith. She believed Michael.

An hour later when he left the convent he carried clothing that would fit Carol. The last detail was a passport. Dressed in her new black habit and wearing large rimmed glasses Carol stood against the closet door while Michael took her picture. Within a few minutes she had altered her current passport. She was now Sister Magdalene Di Conta.

Later that afternoon Michael called a storage company to remove the rest of the furniture in the house and take it to a facility across town. While the truck was backed into the garage and the men carried out the furniture, Carol slipped out of the house and into the van. Hiding in an old trunk that had belong to Michael's mother, she endured the pain of the cramped quarters until the truck pulled up in front of the storage unit. While the men were busy emptying the contents into the storage unit, Michael called them to the front of the truck to pay them, giving Carol time to get out of the trunk and into the building. After unloading everything, they closed the door and locked it. Carol waited in the dark until Michael arrived a few hours later with several more boxes to put in the unit. Although he was not followed, he still made sure that they were careful. Once in Michael's car, Carol lay on the back seat under an old quilt while he drove her back to his house, hopefully for the last time.

When the day finally arrived to depart for Rome, Michael was almost sick to his stomach at the thought of getting through security. What if something went wrong? What would he do?

Just hours before they were to leave, Michael heard someone at the door downstairs. Looking out the bedroom window, he saw Elliott's Escalade parked in the driveway.

"Hey, Meatball, it's me," Elliott yelled out, when he found the door locked. "What's going on with you?"

Michael quickly opened the door. "I was just getting ready to call you. I'm glad you came by," Michael said. "I'm leaving here today."

"What are you doing sitting in this empty house?"

"Just making sure everything is turned off and ready for the new owners. I wish I could say I was going to miss this place, but I'm not."

"So, what are your plans?" Elliott asked.

"I'm escorting some of the nuns from the Sisters of Mercy Convent to Rome and I'm going to visit my mother. They were the ones that arranged for her to stay in the convent in Rome, so I thought I might as well repay the favor since I was going anyway. I'm only going to stay about a week and then I'm heading to Los Angeles."

"What are you going to do out there? Do you have any job prospects?"

"No, but I am sure I'll find something. I just feel it would be better for me to make a fresh start somewhere other than here. I'm going to miss you, Elliott, you've been a good friend to me."

"Don't worry, Meatball, I'll be out there to visit you as soon as you get settled. I already told my father that it might be a while before I go to work for him. Right now, he is acting so weird I really don't want to be around him. He asked me the other day what you were going to do and I told him I didn't know. It was kind of strange. He never asked about you before. I guess it was because of your dad."

Michael looked at his watch. "I have to call a city van. My car won't hold all those women. I'd better do that right now."

"I got a better idea. You take my Escalade and I'll take your car. You can just leave it at the airport and I'll have some-one pick it up."

"Thanks. That will help a lot." He walked Elliott to the door and handed him the keys to his car. He wanted to scream after him, "Your bastard father killed my father, what do you think of that, my friend?" instead he accepted the hug that Elliott gave him.

With Elliott's car parked safely in the garage and out of sight of the blue sedan parked down the street, Carol climbed into the back seat and lay down on the floor. She was already dressed in the black dress and veil.

At the convent, Sister Mary Rose had orchestrated a chaotic scene straight out of a Charlie Chaplin movie. While some of the sisters climbed in the car, others surrounded the car. Two of the sisters got out of the car and then three got back in. At one point, even Michael lost count. Finally with four safely inside the vehicle and Carol sitting up in the back seat, they departed. The ladies in the car laughed with delight at their perfect deception knowing that their movements were being monitored.

Michael dropped the Sisters of Mercy and Carol off in front of the airport and told them to go inside and wait for him. He then proceeded to the long term parking area.

"Someone will pick this car up, but I'm not sure when. It may be a day or two," he said to the parking attendant.

"That's okay, but I need to see your license and registration." Michael pulled his wallet out of his pocket and handed his license to him. "It's not my car, it's belongs to a friend of mine," he said as he leaned across and opened the glove box. Fumbling around to find the registration, he removed a folded brown envelope and placed it on the seat. "Here it is," he said. As the attendant wrote down the information, Michael glanced at the envelope. In the right-hand corner was the name F. Charpelli. It was something from his father. Curious, Michael opened the flap and pulled out one of the papers. It was the papers! The papers that everyone was looking for! There were thin sheets of onionskin paper, with columns of figures and names written on them. His hand began to shake. He wondered what they were doing in Elliott's car. Did Elliott know everything that was going on, if so, why would he be so foolish as to leave the papers in his car?

A gruff voice jarred him. "What?" Michael asked.

"For the third time, I said everything is okay? You can leave the car." The attendant handed him back the registration, which he placed back in the glove box. He folded the envelope and stuffed it into his pocket. His plan had just become a little more complicated.

Once on the airplane, Carol sat a few rows behind him. She pretended to sleep to keep from answering any questions from the others, although they were all engrossed in their bibles.

Michael closed his eyes, yet he knew he couldn't rest. His mind was flooded with complete confusion. *What am I doing? I'm not even twenty-four years old yet and I am running around the country involved in something that could get me killed.* His hand reached into his jacket pocket to once again make sure the papers were still there. *I should be having fun and lots of sex and starting a new career. This is all bullshit. What do I do about Elliott? I can't tell him and when he finds out he is going to hate me, but should I care? His old man is a murdering bastard. And what should I do about Carol and what do I do with these papers? I can't think straight. I have to get a drink.* He signaled for the stewardess and ordered a double scotch on the rocks.

Renting a car at the airport in Rome, Michael and his entourage drove straight to the convent. He was anxious to see his mother.

Rosa was sitting near the window when he lightly knocked on the side of the open door. When she looked up, she let a quiet scream. "Michael, my Michael, oh goodness it is so good that you are here. I have been waiting ever since I got your message." He tried not to seem surprised at her appearance. Dressed in a simple black dress her body had shrunk to an almost anorexic shape. Streaks of gray ran through her once jet black hair and deep lines crossed her forehead making her look so much older than she really was.

Michael bent down and kissed her on the forehead. "Mom, it's so good to see you. I have missed you so much." He hugged her frail body. He knelt down in front of her. "Are you okay, Mom, you look so thin?"

"I'm fine, Michael. I don't have much of an appetite anymore. I eat enough to keep me alive. How long will you be here?' she asked changing the subject.

"About a week and then I am going to Los Angeles. I can't stay in New York anymore. Too many memories for me to handle right now."

Rosa touched her heart. "I brought mine with me. I wish sometimes I could have left them behind, but I wanted to remember all the good times I had with your father."

After a two-hour visit, Michael once again kissed her and told her he would see her in the morning. He had to find a place for Carol to stay where she would be safe. He remembered a place his father talked about called Ravenna. He said it was beautiful there. When he told Carol of his plan, she completely surprised him. "I would like to stay here, Michael, in the convent. While you were visiting with your mother, I had a visit from Mother Angela. She is a very astute woman. I told her that I needed time to cleanse my soul. It will give me time to compile some more information for you."

"My mother doesn't need you around her!" Michael said angrily. "You have done enough to our family."

Carol's eyes filled with tears. "I know I can never undo or even come close to making your mother happy again, but at least, Michael, let me try."

"What about a visa? You're only supposed to be here for a five day visit."

"I'll take care of that and I have some other business to finish also. I just have to do some work on my laptop."

Michael pointed his finger at her. "I'm warning you, Miss Grey, if you cause my mother any grief, I will be the one you will have to hide from."

Thousands of miles away in a zoo in the United States a female elephant named Ella, rocks back and forth in the small enclosure that has been her home for the last seventeen years. When Ella was just a small calf and a member of the herd that was led by Bayanni, the elephants had been scattered when gunshots rained down on them from a low flying helicopter. Her mother lay dead beside her. Ella was captured, put in a crate and transported to a village. Her captor's plans to sell her were foiled when the game warden heard about her. She was confiscated and eventually ended up in the zoo. Frightened and alone, her future was planned for her. Now Ella spent her days in the confines of the outdoor area and her nights in a concrete space with bars on the windows. Her mind still held the memories of her mother and the Savannah where she spent her first seven months. Ella sometimes wept for her lost life and her even bleaker future.

Chapter Nineteen

On his last day in Rome, Michael walked with his mother in the gardens. She held on tightly to his arm. "I am going to miss you. It has been so nice having you here with me."

"When I get a house and things settle down, I want you to come back to the states and live with me. You'll like California. It's sunny all the time."

"Maybe later on, Michael. Right now I would rather stay here. I have peace. I am not happy, but I have peace. I hope you understand."

"I do, and I love you, Mom."

After saying goodbye to all the sisters and thanking them for their help, Michael once more met with Carol in the day room. She looked different now. She still wore the same black dress, but her face had softened somewhat. Perhaps it was a sense of relief that knowing at least for a short time she was out of Garrett's reach. Her hand rested on a brown collapsible folder that was lying in front of her. "Open it," she said, pushing it across the table.

Michael opened the folder and dumped the contents on the table. Picking up the first document he saw his face looking back at him from a passport with the name on it. There was also a California driver's license that had the same picture in the corner.

A social security card, a visa card and a bankbook all carried the name of Jackson Brown.

"What is going on? I'm not going to change my identity. Why would I have to do that?"

"Only for one day, Michael. Just the day you walk into the First Federal Bank in Los Angeles and pick up twenty-seven million dollars. You'll need to buy a fireproof metal case with a combination lock on it."

"How…what…?"

"I know, it's a lot to take in, but everything is all set up for you. When I took the money out of the overseas account set up for your father, I transferred it into a bank in California. I couldn't put it in your father's name. Garrett would have found it in a heartbeat. So instead I created Jackson Brown. And that Michael, will be you. The bank manager will give you the cash and that is the end of it for him. He made a nice amount of money off of it while it was in one of his overseas banks and he is ready to have it gone. And no one will know where it went—only you and me. Who knows when you may need to change your identity? Hold on to all this information. It may come in handy. "

"But, won't they think it's unusual for a single man to come into their bank and walk out with that much money?"

"It's an international bank, Michael. They are used to large transactions. You see, armed guards just draw attention so a lot of the withdrawals are made by a single person. This is an exceptionally large withdrawal but not out of line for them. I have already notified them that you will be making the withdrawal."

Michael shook his head. "I must say, Miss Grey, you missed your calling. The FBI would have been lucky to get you. So, all I have to do is walk in the bank with the case and they will give me twenty-seven million dollars."

"Yes. Do not engage them in conversation, just present this document," she said, pointing to a very official looking letter. "I have also compiled a list of everything I could think of about Garrett and his cohorts—the aliases they use and their screen names. I wish you the best of luck, Michael. In the coming months we can strip Garrett's other secret accounts if he doesn't get smart enough to move them. By the time we are finished with him he will be penniless. Thank you for giving my life back to me."

Michael's hand was trembling. "I hate to admit this, but I'm scared. I'm real scared. When I was angry all I could think about was killing Garrett. I wanted revenge and I still do, but I just don't know how I am going to be able to figure this all out by myself. I know Garrett will have people on me as soon as I return to the states. How am I going to get around all of that?" He rubbed his hands across his forehead. Skydiving out of an airplane into the jungles of Caracas seemed like a piece of cake compared to what lay in front of him.

"You have a right to be scared, Michael. " Carol paced across the marble floor. "I do have one suggestion. I've racked my brain all night trying to remember everything I could about the earlier days at Ferrell. There is a man named Taylor Rhinehart that may be able to help you. Mr. Rhinehart was a detective with the New York Police Department. He had several run ins with Garrett and I think Garrett had him kicked off the force. All I remember is that Mr. Rhinehart really hated Garrett and I think he was an honest man. It's a long shot, Michael, but he may be able to help you. He's now a private investigator but I don't know where. I haven't thought about him in years."

"Are you telling me the truth?" he asked.

"Yes, I swear I am telling you the truth, just like everything else I told you was the truth." Or was it?

Hidden deep in the grove of lush grass the elephants lazily spent the day feeding. The cool evenings kept the insects at bay giving their skin time to heal. Life was good for the elephants. The young calves played close to their mothers while the juveniles tested their prowess against their peers. It was a good time. For now...

Chapter Twenty

Where do you hide twenty-seven million dollars? Under the bed? In a closet? Michael had no idea what to do with the silver case that contained the stacks of large denomination bills. Getting it was easy. Once his nerves had calmed he was able to walk into the bank in Los Angeles and the transaction went smoothly. Walking out was another story. He could imagine men in black suits ready to grab him or policemen lined up with their guns trained on him. None of that happened.

Now he paced around the two-bedroom apartment he had rented looking for a place to stash his money. Putting that much money in one bank was impossible for him and spreading it out in a lot of banks would mean a big headache.

Michael had made quite a few major decisions in the last week. He felt that his mother and Carol were safe in the convent and that eased his mind. There was no way he wanted to go after Garrett right now. He had to get his bearing. He needed his nerves to calm down.

He poured himself a cup of coffee and sat down at the table on his small balcony. With the newspaper spread out in front of him, he soaked up the California sun. The ringing of his cell phone startled him. Who would be calling him here?

"Hey, Meatball, how's it going," Elliott asked. "How's life in California?"

"Good, so far it's pretty good," Michael replied, relieved to hear Elliott's voice.

"You working yet?"

"No, still trying to find something that interests me."

"Well, whatever makes you happy. How about money? You need any?" Elliott asked.

"I got a few thousand left. It should hold me for a while. I'm living a meager existence." He hoped that answer would filter back to Elliott's father.

"I'm going to Amsterdam, Michael. My father has a company there and I am going there to work for a while."

"You don't sound very excited," Michael said.

"Actually, I'm not. There is something going on in my father's company that I don't think he wants me to know about right now, so he is sending me out of the country. But it's probably a good thing. My parents are still in the middle of a bitch of a divorce. My mother wants to take everything she can and he is fighting her all the way. I'd rather not get in the middle of it."

"You never told me they were getting a divorce. Did it just come up?"

"My mother found out he's been keeping some bimbo in an apartment downtown and she hit the roof. Hell, it's not the first time. He's always had other women in his life. I think my mother is pissed because this one is costing him a pretty penny. Anyway, it's a good time to escape from it all. You take care of yourself and I'll give you a call later."

It was tough talking to Elliott. Michael had a hard time keeping his feelings about Elliott's father from seeping into the conversation. It still wasn't time yet. It sounded to him like Garrett was still having problems with his illegal business. That was good and the fact that his wife was on his butt was also good. Poor bastard deserved everything he got.

Michael sat on the stool in the sandwich shop and read his paper while he ate his hamburger. He was engrossed in an article about investment banking, when someone asked, "Is this seat taken?"

He could smell her perfume before he even turned his head. "No," he said, removing his jacket from the stool next to him. She put her briefcase on the floor beneath her feet and slid onto the seat. She smiled at him and he smiled back. *Good-looking woman—older than me, maybe thirty. Nice legs and I love her perfume. Maybe I should talk to her, but she's busy reading the menu. I'll wait a few minutes.*

"The hamburgers are good," he said and then regretted saying it. It sounded stupid. Why else would he be eating it?

"Thanks, but I don't eat meat. I think I'm just going to have a salad."

"Oh," was all he could think of to say.

"I haven't seen you here before," she said. "I eat here almost every day. Service is good and I can usually get by for less than ten dollars for lunch."

What do you know? She is making conversation with me. "I just moved to L.A. a couple of weeks ago from New York." He signaled for the waitress. "Except for the change in the weather it's about as bad out here as it is in New York. I mean the masses of people and the cost of everything."

"My name is Sheila Glass," she said, extending her hand.

"Michael Charpelli, I'm glad to meet you, Sheila."

They talked through her salad and his third glass of iced tea. She was an agent for a mortgage banking company. When he said it sounded interesting to him, she became animated and told him that it was an exciting career. She had to run, but she gave Michael her business card. He wondered it she meant for him to call her or was she just being professional.

Two days later he took the card off of the refrigerator and dialed the number. "Hello, Shelia, this is Michael Charpelli."

On their third date, Shelia spent the night at Michael's apartment. He hadn't expected it, but it was a pleasant surprise.

Shelia was thirty-two and not at all bothered by their age difference. She had been married for a short time when she was much younger and when it didn't work out she decided she wanted to be a career woman. Marriage and babies were not in her future.

She loved her job and right now she was also enthralled with Michael. She was so easy to talk to and so open about everything that he found himself wanting to tell her about his life before he came to California. He wanted to tell her about his family and his hate for Garrett Ferrell and about the millions of dollars under the bed she was sitting on, but something held him back. What if she was a spy Garrett sent after him to find out if he had the papers? He decided to wait.

Shelia sat on the bed with her legs tucked under her, drinking a glass of orange juice. She wore only her bikini underwear and the white shirt Michael had worn the night before. The newspaper was spread out in front of her. "Look at this, Michael," she said. "Here's a house in Pasadena selling for over a million dollars. I can't believe they will get a million for the neighborhood it's in." She continued to scan the paper, while he got dressed. "Now, here," she said, tapping a bold print article, "This is really a good deal for someone if they had some money. Bell Construction bought an office building near Mansard Boulevard. They ran out of money before they could finish turning it into condos. It's in foreclosure."

"How do you know it's a good deal?" Michael asked.

"That's my job, Michael. I know all about foreclosures. Someone will probably buy it and make twenty upscale condos out of the five floors and sell them for between five hundred thousand and seven hundred thousand. That's around ten million bucks if they all sell."

"How much does someone need to take over the foreclosure?" he asked out of curiosity.

"Six million."

He feigned a laugh. "Way out of my ballpark. Let's go get some breakfast."

After he dropped Shelia off at her office, Michael called the number listed in the paper. He made an appointment to see the bank officer, Michael Gaines, who was handling the foreclosure. Telling Mr. Gaines that he was a representative for a prospective buyer. Michael took a tour of the building and by the end of the day told Mr. Gaines, he would have a cashier check for the down payment ready for him the next day. He would reinvent the alias Carol had given him—just long enough to get his hands on the property.

In the next month with Shelia's keen business sense for finding prospective property, Michael purchased two more buildings and spent a total of eight million dollars in the name of Jackson Brown. He now had a legal business with some of the money invested and the rest distributed in four different banks. He was a property owner and stood to make a handsome profit. That same month he approached Shelia about finding him a house. The apartment was closing in on him. He wanted a larger place. Shelia was excited and started the search sending him tons of emails on property for sale. He was stunned by the prices. "Hey, you're living in one of the most expensive cities on the northern continent," Shelia said, laughing at his response to the cost of housing.

When he finally settled on a three-bedroom ranch in Venice, Shelia threw her arms around his neck and kissed him. "Oh, I love you, Michael, you just gave me a big commission check." And along with the commission check he gained a roommate. Shelia moved in with him three days after he closed on the house.

Michael hated lying to Shelia, but it kept her safe. When he told her he was working for a man named Jackson Brown, she didn't question him. Life was getting better by the day for both of them. Their nights of passion were followed by days when they seemed like little more than friends. With each of them busy working on their careers there was little time for long languid weekends. In the evenings they ate dinner together and talked about business or they sat at their computers hardly talking to each other. Yet for right now, it seemed to work. She was not one to pry into his past and he left well enough alone, not asking her too many questions. He liked her, he liked her a lot, but he really couldn't call it love. What had happened in his life was never far from the front of his mind and he still wasn't comfortable talking to her about it.

Jakuta wandered into a place he had never been before. Taking a detour around the washed-out gully, he ended up in a narrow rift cut deep into the Savannah. The closed in feeling of the narrow walls made him nervous. Backing up, he decided to take another path. He was unaware of the poachers sitting on the hood of their camouflaged truck until he was almost upon them. They seemed as startled as he was when he came out of the crevasse right in front of them. Unable to get to their guns quickly enough, Jakuta trotted past them and headed toward the cover of the bush. He had been too clever for them.

Chapter Twenty-One

Taylor Rhinehart flipped through his appointment book. The name Michael Charpelli was penciled in for a three o'clock appointment. Taylor did not like surprises. It only took him a few hours to find out everything he needed to know about Michael Charpelli. What concerned him most was the name Ferrell Enterprises connected to Mr. Charpelli's name.

Michael arrived promptly at 3 o'clock and was annoyed that he was kept waiting for twenty minutes. When he was finally shown into Taylor's office his displeasure was evident. Taylor stood up and extended his hand but made no apology for keeping Michael waiting. It was his edge. He always liked to have the upper hand on his first meeting with a new client. Sitting down, he motioned to the chair in front of his desk. Michael sat and purposely dropped his brief case to the floor with a hefty slam.

"So, Mr. Charpelli, let's get right down to business. What is the reason you need a private investigator? Are you in trouble with the law?"

"No, I'm not in trouble. I'm looking for trouble, big trouble and I need someone to help me make it happen."

His response intrigued Taylor. "Really. Well, let's get down to business. I'm a private investigator, not a miracle worker or a bounty hunter. I work on an hourly basis, with all my expenses covered. At any time you feel I am not giving you what you want, you can discontinue the use of my service. Are we clear?'

Michael nodded.

"Okay then, what is it you want me to do?"

"I'm very nervous about what I'm about to tell you and I have to make sure you understand that anything I tell you is strictly confidential."

"That, Mr. Charpelli is a given."

Michael opened his brief case and laid several thin sheets of paper on his desk. "It's all about these." He tapped on the papers. "My father was killed because of these papers and I know who did it. My problem is trying to prove it. The bastard I'm after is named Garrett Ferrell. Ever heard of him?" Once again, Michael repeated his story of his father's death.

"I have four people that I would like for you to investigate for me," Michael said. "The first one is fairly easy. Her name is Shelia Glass. She lives in Los Angeles. Actually she lives with me. I want to know everything about her. I am ninety-nine percent sure she is who she says she is, but right now, I have to be one hundred percent sure. I want you to find out if she is in contact with anyone in New York. I feel guilty for what I am doing to Shelia, but right now I can't take any chances that anyone I meet might be working for Garrett. The second person is Garrett Ferrell. I want to know what's going on in his life right now. I'm not concerned about his past. I want to know who he is seeing, what kind of money he's spending, how his company is doing and anything else that you find is pertinent. Then there is Ari Goldman. He worked for Garrett but he disappeared about six months ago. See if anyone knows where he is. The last one may be the hardest to find. It is a man named Howard. I don't even know his last name, but he worked for Garrett, also. I want him found." He handed Taylor the list that Carol had given him. "Here, this will probably help some."

"I'm not sure I can help you, Mr. Charpelli. I've had a few run-ins with Mr. Ferrell in the past. In fact he is on my short list of people I really hate. Actually, we have an enemy in common."

"That's good, then we're on the same page. I want to destroy that bastard and then I want to see him dead. I really need your help, Mr. Rhinehart. I will pay you a lot of money to help me. Without help, I'll never be able to nail him and then he'll walk away a free man once again."

Taylor stood up and extended his hand. "I'll start on it right away."

After Michael left, Taylor sat at his desk and stared out the window at the San Francisco Bay. Garrett Ferrell. He never thought he'd be going after that son of a bitch again. This time he wouldn't get away from him. This time he had enough money to take care of him. Michael's resources were the tools that he had needed for a long time. He had forgotten to ask Michael why he had chosen him to investigate Garrett. It was just too much of a coincidence.

Michael's first report came within one week of his visit with Taylor. It was on Shelia. Everything she had told him about herself was true. Taylor could not find any connection between Shelia and Garrett Ferrell or anyone in his organization. It would be two weeks before he heard from Taylor again.

On the night Michael got Taylor's report on Shelia he decided to relieve his guilt by taking her out to dinner. Looking lovely in a slender black dress, she sat across the table from him and grinned. "I know you are up to something, Michael. This is the first time we've been out on the town in over two months."

"I know, and I'm sorry." He put a blue, velvet box on the table and slid it towards her.

"A present? It's not my birthday." She opened the box and stared at the row of perfect diamonds glistening in the light of the table lamp. "Wow, this is a gorgeous bracelet." She lifted it out of the box and draped it across her wrist. After a moment she put it back into the box. "I can't accept this, Michael. I wish I could, but I have something I have wanted to tell you all week and I guess now is the time to say it. I'm going to be moving out of the house. Before you say a word, let me explain. It has nothing to do with me being unhappy, but I just think I would like to have my own place again."

"Have I done something wrong? Is there someone else?'

She lowered her head. "No, there isn't anyone else and you are an absolute sweetheart. Let's face it, we haven't exactly been head over heels in love with each other. I can tell we're drifting apart. I mean…the sex is good, but you seem so far away from me most of the time. I know you would always take care of me and I could become a kept woman, but I really want to have my own company someday. I need to put all my effort into my career and so do you. I'm sorry, Michael, but I don't believe you are any more in love with me than I am with you. I don't want to hurt your feelings. I really want you to be one of my best friends forever and of course I love doing business with you." She pushed the velvet box toward him.

Michael took her hand. "Keep the bracelet as a symbol of my undying friendship and gratitude for making me a semi-rich man." He kissed her fingers. "I'm glad to have a friend like you, Shelia."

"Then you're not mad?" she asked.

He grinned. "No, not at all. You are a special person and I'm glad you were honest with me. Let's eat, I'm hungry."

That night, as he rolled over to her side of the bed, he gently pushed her hair off her face and kissed her neck. "I'll be honest, this I am going to miss."

She murmured, "Me, too."

The poachers were still on Jakuta's trail. Following him day after day through the bush. Jakuta could smell the sweat from their shirts and hear the sounds of their voices from miles away. He could hear the clatter of the ivory tusks that had been cut off the faces of the elephants as they rattled around in the back of the truck. Finding a thicket covered with inch long thorns from the Mayetta bushes, he hid himself behind the brown brambles. They camouflaged him quite well. The smell of death was all around him, but this time he would not be one of the prey.

Chapter Twenty-Two

Michael took the large brown envelope from the UPS driver and signed his name. Padding across the living room floor in his bare feet, he pulled off the tape. A stack of photographs drifted to the floor. Bending down, he stared into the face of Ari Goldman. Attached to the picture was a note from Taylor. " I have found him. How much do you want to spend to get rid of him?"

Michael made a quick call to Taylor, saying just a few words." Whatever it takes."

That was all Taylor needed. He had a lot of connections but they didn't come cheap. For the right amount of money he could accomplish almost anything.

The other four photos in the envelope were of women that Garrett had been with in the past several years. From what Taylor could ascertain, Garrett preferred high priced call girls that would be willing to see him exclusively until he tired of them. Taylor assumed they knew nothing about his business, but plenty about his personal life. These kinds of women would usually cooperate with anyone who threatened them with jail time. He was sure that Garrett's wife, Marguerite would have her lawyers on their trail as soon as she received the email he was about to send her.

Garrett had a team of lawyers working on his divorce, but according to inside information Garrett's wife, Marguerite was waging a fierce campaign against him. Garrett may end up paying her a huge sum. Garrett was still pleading innocent to adultery in his marriage.

Taylor also said that Garrett's company seemed a little shaky. He had pulled in quite a few of his stock options and the price for each share had dropped sharply. He also found out from an inside source that Garrett had posted a memo to all of the departments that all raises and bonuses were frozen. Many of his employees were resigning due to the cuts in pay and benefits. It seemed to Taylor that Garrett was beginning to feel the pinch.

Taylor had located Ari living in a motel in Florida. The following morning Taylor swung into action. He flew to the Florida Keys where he rented a magnificent yacht in the name of Garrett Ferrell. He gave them a twenty thousand dollar deposit. He then returned to New York and leased a new Mercedes in Garrett's name.

His next move was to send a priority mail envelope to Ari. When it arrived at Ari's house, Ari signed for it and opened it. Inside was a note on Ferrell Enterprises' stationary.

Everything is going well. It would be a good idea if you took a vacation. I have purchased a few things that may make your vacation a little nicer. Stay away until I call you. Iron Man.

A smile crossed Ari's face. He was relieved that Garrett was letting him off the hook for not producing the papers after he and Howard killed Frank. It would be good to get away and relax for a while. Ari looked at the two enclosed documents. One was a bogus bill of sale for the Mercedes that he could pick up at any time and the other the title to the yacht in slip number seventeen at Gulfway Pier in Florida. He let out a whoop and started packing his clothes. Garrett had come through for him after all.

When Taylor was sure that Ari had picked up the car and headed down to the pier he sent a second priority envelope to Garrett's office. When the mail was put on Garrett's desk the envelope caught his eye. It was addressed to Ari and marked personal and confidential. He buzzed his new secretary. "Why did you leave this envelope to Ari on my desk? Take it to his office."

"But, Mr. Goldman is not here, Mr. Ferrell. He called in a few days ago and said he wouldn't be back for some time. I'm sorry, I thought you knew."

"What? Where did he go?"

"I'm sorry, Mr. Ferrell, but he didn't say."

Garrett was seething. How dare that wimp take off without telling him. He grabbed the envelope off his desk and ripped it open. They were two false documents created just for Garrett—a bill of sale for a one hundred and seven thousand dollar Mercedes and two hundred and seventy-five thousand dollars for the yacht. Garrett jumped up from his desk, knocking over his chair. "You little son of a bitch. When I find you, you are dead. You are a dead man, Ari Goldman."

Pacing his office for over an hour and drinking half a bottle of brandy, Garrett grew more anxious as each hour passed. When the door finally opened he threw the glass on the floor and threw the documents across his desk. "I knew that son of a bitch was lying to me. He had those papers all along. He took them out of Frank's pocket. Look at these," he said pointing to the papers. "That bastard is buying cars and yachts in my name."

"Aren't you at all interested in who sent you that information?" Howard asked. "This may all be a setup. I don't think Ari would be this stupid."

"Oh, you don't think so," Garrett said in a mocking tone. Well then, dammit, check it out," Garrett roared, "and then go get him. I want him dead."

Howard heaved his heavy body out of the chair. "Okay, I'll leave right away. He turned and pointed his finger at Garrett. "This better be on the level or you'll have to deal with me. I don't want to be walking into no trap."

"Get out! Get out!" Garrett shouted. He did not like the lumbering ass threatening him.

Ari let out a low whistle when he came in view of the white yacht bobbing in the water. It was huge. Yeah, just like Garrett to buy something so big., Ari thought. Hell there was no way he could manage this thing by himself. He didn't have enough money to hire a staff. Oh, well, there were a few nice restaurants and lounges just a block away. He would just relax on the boat and have a good time. He really needed to unwind.

Ari took a tour of the yacht and then stood on the deck looking out into the ocean. He grinned as two bikini clad women sauntered down the dock. Yeah, he could get used to this kind of life. He didn't pay any attention to the smaller boat docked next to him in slip sixteen or to the fake parrot hanging on the rail with the tiny hole in his belly—just big enough for the lens of a camera.

The wetlands just below the rim of the Mandingo ridge was reserved for the predators of the Savannah. Giant croco-

diles that lay in wait for their prey, enormous hippos that hid just below the surface of the water and the ever present snakes that slithered silently through the water. Even with his size and girth on his side, Jakuta was weary of the watery expanse, yet he needed to drink. He would not take time to bathe in this place.

Chapter Twenty-Three

Howard did not like boats. He did not even like walking on the piers that led to the yachts. The movement made him nauseated, but if this little venture turned out right Garrett would reward him with a nice chunk of money.

Howard had taken an afternoon flight and rented a car at the airport. It was a forty-mile drive to the ocean. The Gulf Way Marina was off the beaten path and surrounded on three sides by low water and marshland. He wondered how Ari had even found it. Howard sat down at an outside bar over looking the marina. He ordered a beer and turned on the stool to get a good look at the layout. Slot seventeen was in plain sight. He sipped on his beer and watched for any movement on the deck. There were people meandering up and down the pier. Howard had just finished his third beer when Ari appeared on the deck of the yacht for just a second and then went back down below. It was almost dark and the dock was now empty. Time to make his move.

Howard flicked his cigarette into the water and cautiously walked down the narrow gangplank leading to Ari's yacht. Sweat poured off his face as he tried to keep his balance. He crawled over the railing and waited a moment until the rocking motion had stopped. "Ari, hey, Ari, you in there?" he said in a slurred voice as he tried to see down the stairs into the cabin.

"Who is it?" came a startled voice from below.

"It's me, Howard." Howard held onto the sides of the tapered steps as he slowly descended into the cabin. "Hey, old Buddy, how are you?"

He caught Ari completely off guard. "What are you doing here? How did you find me?" Ari asked in a surprised voice.

"Garrett sent me. He is pretty pissed at you for disappearing like you did and then buying that car and this boat in his name. I'll tell you one thing, Ari, you sure got some balls. I'll make this quick. Give me the papers and you can sail out to sea in your little boat."

"Dammit, I don't have the papers. What's this all about?"

"You're repeating yourself, Ari. Now, I know you have what I want, so just hand them over and let's be done with this." He pulled his pistol out from his inside coat pocket.

"Look I'm supposed to be hiding out. I have no idea why you're here. If I had them I would have given them to Garrett and got myself off the hook. Garrett gave me the car and boat. Just call him up and he'll tell you. Now put the gun away." Ari was beginning to whine. He wiped the back of his hand across his forehead. "Garrett must be going nuts. He knows I don't have enough money to buy a yacht like this."

"That's a crock of crap. Garrett never bought you a damn thing. All I know is that you and I have to work this out some way since you're not being very cooperative."

Howard looked out the window, his gun still trained on Ari. "I hear there are alligators that live in the marshland around here—big ones, maybe twelve foot long. They're hungry all the time. I wonder if I hung a piece of raw meat around your waist and lowered you half way into the water if they would come for lunch?" Howard opened the refrigerator. "Well, lookee here. I bet the gators would love this steak. Take your pants off Ari."

Ari had to contemplate his next move. He slowly backed away from Howard and held on to the overhead rail for leverage. He could tell that Howard had been drinking. "I ain't taking off my pants. Pointing toward the door he yelled, Hey, Howard, look out behind you!'

Howard jerked his head sideways and Ari lunged forward knocking him off balance. He ran for the steps just as Howard steadied himself and grabbed Ari by the legs. Kicking and screaming, Ari rolled over and punched Howard in the face. With blood running from his nose, Howard put his arm around Ari's head and smashed his face into the metal bed frame. Ari let out a moan and his body went limp. Dropping him to the floor, Howard grabbed a towel from the sink and held it to his nose. "You son of a bitch, you broke my nose." There was no answer from Ari. Howard nudged him with his shoe. Ari did not move. "Aw, crap," Howard said. He knew that Ari was dead and he still didn't have the papers. Maybe he could make it look like an accident, like Ari got himself drunk and fell overboard.

Picking up his limp body Howard heaved it over his shoulder and stumbled up the steps still holding the towel on his nose. With a resounding splash, Ari's body hit the water. Howard took the grappling pole from the railing and pushed the body under the bow.

Howard needed to search the boat, but right now he had to get his throbbing nose taken care of. He would come back later. Walking up the gangplank, Howard made his film debut in front of Taylor's surveillance cameras with a swollen nose and a blood stained shirt. He had made a big mistake. He should have left the body on the yacht. An anonymous call to the shore patrol was all it took. They found Ari's body hooked on the blade of the motor and the boat was impounded.

When Howard saw the shore patrol pulling into the pier he knew that Garrett would be livid that he didn't find the papers.

Still holding his throbbing nose, Howard decided it was time for him to disappear, too.

ঌ ঌ ঌ ঌ

Taylor looked at the check Michael had just handed him. "Sorry I couldn't get you more information on Garrett Ferrell. He is a pretty elusive person. He covers himself real good. It was just luck that I got hold of those pictures."

"That's okay," Michael replied. "At least you got one of the bastards that killed my father. What did you find out about this Howard guy?"

"Well I got him on film. I'll keep the pictures under raps for a while and see if he shows up. He went by the name Howard Notch, but his real name is Chez Balavera. He has a rap sheet a mile long and has been in prison twice. He has a sister living in Tequila and a brother in Vahuevo. Both said they hadn't seen him in years. When I told them that I had a check for Chez, they perked up a little bit. I offered them each ten thousand dollars if they could find him and let me know without telling him. It's a slim chance, Michael, but these people are pretty poor. I'll keep on it." Taylor folded the check and put it in his pocket. As he walked down the driveway to his car, he wondered why such a young man like Michael would want to take on Garrett Ferrell.

Michael closed the door and walked into the kitchen. He put three ice cubes in a glass and filled it half full with bourbon. In the living room he sat down in front of the window and stared at the amazing California sunset.

His father had been on his mind all afternoon. He wondered how scared his father was when he knew he was going to die. How cruel were Ari and Howard before they hung him? Did his father cry and beg for mercy? Were his father's last thoughts of his mother and him? Michael hurled the glass and it smashed against the window. Streaks of brown bourbon marred the beautiful California sunset.

The young female had just turned thirteen years of age. Leaving the confines of the herd, she circled around to the outside rim. She had heard the grunts and rumblings of the males nearby. It was her first season in estrus. She would let it be known that she was ready to be courted.

Chapter Twenty-Four

"I'm going to be in Los Angeles next week," Elliot said. "We're going to celebrate your birthday, Meatball. I've rented a beach house at Malibu for the week."

"You could at least say hello. When did you get back from Amsterdam?" Michael asked.

"Last week and I am ready to party. My apartment is in a shambles since my mother has decided to stash half her crap here while I was away. She's trying to keep my father from taking all her stuff. They are really going at it. Somebody sent some incriminating pictures to my mother's lawyer that is making her very happy and my father even angrier. So, what better excuse to leave town than your birthday? I have to run. I'll see you in a couple of days."

Michael was in no mood to party or even to see Elliott. He wasn't sure he wanted to continue his friendship with him much longer. The tendrils of mistrust were growing around Michael everyday. So far, Elliott had not given him one hint to suggest that he knew anything about the mess his father had created. He was hoping that Carol Grey was wrong and that Garrett would keep Elliott out of it.

Elliott arrived at Michael's house two days later. He looked tan and rested and not at all like someone who had spent four months in Amsterdam. Elliott gave a low whistle when he walked through the living room. "Hey, this is some place. I like your stuff. Great leather couches. You pick all this out?"

"No, Shelia decorated the whole place. She had good taste."

"Sorry, things didn't work out with you two, but what the hell, we're young, we got a lot of time to settle down." Elliott continued to walk around the room and opened the door to the patio. "Nice, really nice. So I assume you are doing okay? Have you made your first million yet?"

"Actually, I've made a couple. I work from home, so I have very little overhead. Shelia helps me locate the properties, my contractors fix them up and then we sell as fast as we can to keep from making big mortgage payments. Anything half way decent goes real fast in this area, especially if you keep it priced right."

"Listen to you. You sound like an old real estate pro." Elliott changed the subject. Maybe he did not like the idea that Michael was really succeeding in something and he was still hanging on his father's coat tails. "Anyway, I want to make sure you have no plans for the weekend. Your birthday party starts on Saturday, but who knows, it may last until Sunday."

"Am I going to know anyone at my party besides you?" Michael asked.

"Maybe a few guys from school who live in L.A. The rest will probably be from around the area. You know, say the word party and they'll come. You don't have to bring a date, you can have your pick of the beach girls," Elliott said, laughing.

The whole thing sounded very juvenile to Michael. They talked for a couple of hours, Elliott drinking half a bottle of bourbon and still insisting he could drive when he got ready to leave. After three attempts he was able to get out of the lounge chair on the patio and stagger to the door. "Sorry, bud, I'm calling you a cab," Michael said.

Elliott swayed back and forth, "Even on my worst day I am better than you on your best day and don't you forget that," He hiccupped twice and then fell flat on his face. He left the next morning with a throbbing headache and little recollection of the night before.

Cleaning up the mess on the patio, it suddenly occurred to Michael that maybe Elliott had forgotten all about putting the papers in the glove compartment of his car. He was really drunk on the day of the funeral.

Michael could hear the blaring music when he turned onto the beach road leading to the house Elliott had rented. People were everywhere; and Michael never recognized anyone. He gave his keys to the valet and bumped his way through the crowd to the back of the house. Elliott was talking to a group of people by the pool. When he saw Michael he waved to him. "Hey, everyone, here comes the birthday boy," Elliott yelled out, but no one seemed to care much. The booze was flowing easy tonight and the smell of marijuana filled the air. Meeting him halfway, Elliott motioned toward the bar that had been setup by the pool, "Get yourself a drink. This is a hell of a party. I'll be back in a minute."

Michael managed to strike up a conversation with a few people in the next hour, but the music was so loud it was hard to talk. He wandered inside the house, but it was not much better with people crowded into every corner. Dodging spilt drinks and women who wanted to kiss the birthday boy, Michael escaped out the patio door and found a corner at the bottom of the outside stairs. Sipping his drink he watched as several people began stripping off their clothes and jumping into the pool, while others waded in fully clothed. Elliott had joined in with them. Michael knew it was time for him to exit before Elliott found him and threw him in the water. He rounded the corner and pressed himself against the marble rail while three naked bodies ran passed him.

His attention was drawn to the maze of glitters dancing across the marble stairs. The sparkles were radiating from the dress worn by a woman standing in the patio doorway. The lights from the house silhouetted her body. Michael recognized her. He took the three steps to the balcony, trying to think of something to say to her. "Aren't you going to join the fun?" he asked, motioning toward the pool.

She shook her head no. Her finger chased the ice cubes around the glass.

"Why? Too cold for you?" he asked

"No, two thousand dollar dress," she replied.

What could he come back with? He had to think of something quick. Girls like her didn't spend much time conversing with guys like him.

"Do you need another drink?" he asked. *That was dumb, her glass was almost full.*

Once again she shook her head. "No, I've had enough of this place. What I need right now is a ride home. Do you have a car?"

"Ah…yes…sure I have a car." He fumbled in his pocket and held up his keys as proof to her that he had a car. *Another dumb move.*

She followed a few steps behind him as he made his way down the balcony steps trying to dodge the sprays of water coming from the pool. "I better say goodnight to Elliott before I leave."

"Me too," she answered.

Above the din of noise from the people in the water, Michael cupped his hands and called to Elliott, with no luck.

She put two fingers in her mouth and let out a shrill whistle, which got everyone's attention. She waved to Elliott.

Climbing out of the pool, he shook the water off his hair. She seemed unmoved by his naked body. "I'm leaving," she said.

"Yeah, me too, Elliott. I'm going to give her a ride home."

"Why are you two leaving so early? The party is just beginning to kick into high gear. Why not stick around and do a couple of lines. I got some premium stuff in the house."

"Call me later." She turned and started toward the driveway.

Elliott grinned at Michael. "Maybe you'll get lucky tonight."

"I'm just giving her a ride home. That's all."

"Yeah, I bet," Elliott turned and jumped back in the water. He was too drunk to care about them.

She was standing on the edge of the driveway smoking a cigarette when he caught up with her. He handed his keys to the valet.

"My name is Michael Charpelli."

"Shay Young," she answered. She didn't have to tell him, he already knew.

The valet opened the door to the red Mazarati and she slipped in. "Nice car," she said. "Take the Pacific Highway toward Granite Canyon."

"You're Elliott's friend from college," she commented.

He nodded, " And you're Shay Young, the super model. I've seen your picture on almost every fashion magazine in the airport."

She did not respond. *Another stupid statement on his part.*

"Actually, I've met you once before," he said. "We were at some party in New York and you were with Elliott. He introduced me to you. You had on a red dress."

"You have a good memory. I was probably so out of it that I wouldn't have recognized myself if I looked in the mirror." She laid her head on the headrest and closed her eyes.

"I suppose I should have stayed since I was the guest of honor," he said, wanting to break the silence.

"Me too," she added. "I was his date."

She was quiet the rest of the drive and he couldn't think of anything to say.

"Turn right at the next corner. The first drive on the right is mine."

Michael easily maneuvered his car up the steep incline leading to the top of the canyon.

Her house was an expensive, white stucco, nestled in a grove of trees just feet from the edge of a steep precipice. The front of the house facing the canyon was a wall of windows.

She didn't wait for him to help her out of the car. She got out and opened her purse, fumbling for her keys. "Would you like to come in? I can fix you a drink or something to eat?"

"A drink would be fine." His mouth was dry.

Shay turned on the lights in the black and white room and kicked off her shoes. "I'll be just a minute," she said as she crossed the white, plush rug and started down the dimly lit hall. He watched as she pulled the sequined dress over her head. A thin strand of material from her thong interrupted the long line of her back. She returned a few minutes later in a pair of blue sweat pants and an oversized tee shirt. "This is much better," she said. "That dress was driving me crazy. I'm glad I borrowed it from wardrobe instead of buying it. Now, what can I fix you?" Her mood had completely changed. "How about some soup? I made it this morning. It's vegetable beef."

Soup! She was offering him soup. That was new one for him. “Sure, sounds pretty good.”

He followed her in the black and white kitchen and sat on a stool by the counter. “Can I help?” he asked as she took bowls and jars out of the refrigerator.

“ No thanks.” She closed the refrigerator with her foot. “I have some great pickles and cheese too.”

Michael let out a small chuckle. “I thought models never ate.”

“Oh I do. Maybe not a lot, but most everything I want. It will probably all catch up with me someday. Besides in about five years I’ll be too old for the runway and probably end up doing infomercials on TV for some sports equipment.”

He looked at her classic face. “Too old? What are you now, about 25?”

“Twenty-eight, she answered. “Fix yourself a drink, if you want?” she said, pointing to a cart laden with crystal decanters.

“Coffee is fine, if you have it,” Michael replied. The soup was good. He ate two bowls full— she ate one. She fished the last of the pickles out of the jar and nibbled on it. She pointed the pickle at Michael. “So you’re the one that does all those crazy things with Elliott every year. You’re his best friend, aren’t you?”

“Are you surprised?” he asked. “Did you expect some-one taller?”

“That was a silly thing to say, Michael. Actually I never thought about you at all. Do you have a hang up about your height?”

“I suppose, being five seven isn’t the greatest. How tall are you? Six foot?”

“I’m five ten, six feet in heels. Are you as rich as Elliott?”

"I am richer than Elliott. Elliott's father is rich, but he isn't. You say what's on your mind, don't you, Shay."

"Only when it's one on one. I'm pretty quiet in public. Paparazzi is always hanging around waiting for me to say or do something dumb. You were lucky they weren't there tonight. Otherwise your picture might be on the front of one of the rag magazines tomorrow. I guess I shouldn't be so blunt, but I usually don't have much time to get to know people."

"What about Elliott? How did you two meet?" Michael asked.

"A long time ago when I just started in modeling. It was at a party. He came right up to me and put his arm around my waist. He really caught me off guard. There was something about him that made me curious about his boldness. Of course, he had everything a girl could want. He was good looking, charismatic and rich." She stood up and took the bowls off the table and placed them in the sink. "Elliott was pretty much of a party person then, but I guess you knew that. He had just come back from your trip to South America. I heard all about the two of you jumping off those really high cliffs. My problem was I had been clean from drugs and alcohol for almost two years and the thought of being with someone who loved to snort made me nervous. I never, and I mean never wanted to be where I was a couple of years before, but within a few weeks after we met it began to happen—too many parties, too many late nights. I forgot all about the hell I had been through getting clean, much less the career moves it cost me. Anyway I was falling back into my old habits when I was with Elliott. Then one night I found myself laying on the ledge of his balcony ready to fall over the edge. He saved me from dying, but I had to give him up to save me from the other death that was consuming me. He was pretty upset when I left. When he called and asked me to come to his party I was really surprised. I can't see that he has changed much."

"Were you in love with him?" Michael asked, not sure she would answer him.

"I'm not sure. It wasn't the heart thumping, I can't wait to see you type of feeling, but I do admit that Elliott has a way with women. And that is the key word, *women.* I don't think he has it in him to be faithful to just one person very long. And of course the drugs and drinking made my decision to leave him pretty easy." Shay stretched her arms over her head, her shirt tightening across her breast. "I'm tired. I need to go to bed. Do you want to stay? I don't mean with me, but I have an extra bedroom if you don't feel like driving home."

"No, I think I'll leave. Thanks for the soup, it was good."

"Do you like pot roast, Michael? I'm going to make one tomorrow. If you get bored, stop by."

She closed the door before he could answer her. She was different for sure, but he liked her attitude.

There was a message on his machine when he woke up around eleven.

"Heard you spent the night with Shay last night, Meatball. Did you get any? I'm about ready to give her up, if you want her. I admit she looked good on my arm, but she is way too serious for me. I'm on my way to bed. The party is over…I think."

The message irritated Michael. *What did Elliott mean…you can have her? That remark sounded like something Garrett would say. Was that the Ferrell men's style? Get tired of people and just get rid of them or give them away. Was Elliott more like his father than Michael really knew? Today he would not dwell on it. He had to get ready to eat roast beef.*

After roast beef, there was leg of lamb on Saturday and then beef tenderloin on Sunday. She was a good cook, even though he would have eaten hot dogs and beans just to be near her. When she off-handedly asked him if he would like to accompany her to Baja for a photo shoot he was surprised.

"Would you have any free time?" he asked.

She bent over his chair. "I'll always find time for you, Michael." He could feel his face turning red. She laughed and tussled his hair. "Go home and pack. We'll leave around noon tomorrow."

Michael sat on the beach next to the layout designer watching the photographer take pictures of Shay. He photographed her romping in the water in a bikini bottom and a flimsy white shirt and laying on the sand in various poses. It wasn't the weather that made Michael sweat. It was the sight of her. She was the most seductive person he had ever seen. When the shoot was over he watched as she poured water over her legs and wiped the oil from her skin. He wanted to bolt from his chair and help her, but he knew that wouldn't be appropriate.

"That was great," he said as she came up and sat down next to him. "Wow, now I know why designers want you in their shows. You got it going on."

She smiled at him. "Let's go back to the hotel. I'll change and then we can go eat."

Food was not what Michael had on his mind, but he followed her lead. They ate on the balcony of the hotel. She wore a white dress with her hair held in place by a red scarf. She looked great to him. Shay drank two glasses of wine with dinner and began to giggle. She leaned across the table and took Michael's hand. "I really like you, Michael. You are so different than anyone I have ever met." She took the last swallow from the glass. "You make me comfortable. You make me want to tell you things that you really don't need to know and you love my cooking."

"I hope that is a compliment, Shay. I'm beginning to feel like one of your girlfriends."

She giggled again, running her fingers up his arm. "Oh, no, not tonight. Tonight you are my handsome lover. Tonight I want you to take me upstairs and into my bed and make love to me like I was the first girl you ever touched."

"I can do that," Michael groaned. It was going to be difficult to get out of the chair.

She opened the door to her room and he stepped inside behind her. She turned and he took her into his arms. She smelled like lavender. He kissed her tenderly at first and then pulled her close to him. Her tongue counted all his teeth and her body molded against his. Michael backed up, "Wait! Wait, I'll be right back." He made a dash for the bathroom. He stood over the commode groaning. He had to make sure he could last long enough to satisfy her.

When he returned to the bedroom, she lay across the bed naked. The light shining in the window accented the long lines of her body. He undressed quickly and lay down next to her. He gently kissed her back and shoulders. His hands reached around and caressed her breasts. She did not move. She was asleep. He lay there staring at the ceiling feeling completely rejected.

Her apology in the morning more than made up for the night before. By noon they finally decided to get out of bed.

"So, what does all this mean, Shay?" Michael asked.

"Does it have to mean something? Let's not rush things, Michael. Let's just let it happen naturally and not put a name on it. You know I lead a crazy life and it's not easy. Tomorrow I may be half way around the world on another assignment. It would make me crazy if I knew someone was at home wondering about my every move."

He reached over and kissed her. "Fair enough, but if anybody asks, I'll tell them that I love you."

She threw the pillow over his face. "You better not."

He wouldn't really do that, but he did love her. The phone interrupted their playful mood.

"I have good news, Michael. I found Howard. He is living in a small village about eighteen miles from Mexico City. "What do you want me to do?" Taylor asked.

Michael got out of bed and walked outside onto the balcony. He didn't want Shay to hear his conversation. "Can you take care of him? I mean, you know, get him out of the picture and in jail," Michael asked. He had been so busy with Shay that he had put his pursuit of Garrett on the back burner. He had left all the digging to Taylor. "Don't do anything stupid, Taylor. You don't need to be charged with murder for killing scum like him. Mexican jails are hell."

"Oh, he is going to die, all right, but it won't be me that kills him. Thanks, I'll get back to you."

Languishing in the cool water of the lakes formed by the rainy season, Jakuta freed himself of the mud that was caked to his feet and making it difficult for him to walk. He lowered his head beneath the water and let the soothing liquid cleanse his eyes and ears. He was at peace. For now the poachers had moved out of the area and the herds of females would be making their way to the watering holes—females who would be receptive to mating. He was in good form now. At twenty-five years of age and weighing almost eight tons his stamina surpassed the older bulls and his size discouraged the younger bulls. They had to wait their turn. Jakuta was as strong as a bulldozer who could modify the landscape by his mere presence.

Chapter Twenty-Five

Garrett Ferrell sat at his normally neat desk that was now littered with papers and folders. For three weeks he had been evading the calls and emails from his overseas clients. They were ready to resume business and they were not willing to wait much longer. He wondered how risky it would be to take them on again. Turning toward his computer screen he scrolled down the list of over ninety emails. One immediately caught his attention. The words, *Did my job. Need money. Iron man.* Garrett knew it was from Howard. He grinned. Time to tie up some loose ends. He typed in the word. *Okay.*

Did his job, who did he think he was kidding? Garrett had read all about Ari's death in the newspaper. He had even been questioned by several agents about Ari's possible association with the underworld. They asked him about the yacht and the Mercedes which were both in Garrett's name. Garrett said that he often lent his employees his personal possessions, but in this instance he had no idea that Ari had taken them without his permission. Actually Garrett had no idea what they were talking about. What yacht? What Mercedes? They showed him a picture of the man leaving the yacht and he held back his surprise when he recognized Howard. He said he had never seen the man before. And yes, he was worried that Ari was doing something illegal. There were funds missing from the company that he was having investigated. They left satisfied with his answers.

The back and forth banter between Garrett and who he thought was Howard continued all week over the Internet. Information about Ari and other things written in the code that Carol had given to Michael was doing what they had hoped. It made Garret comfortable enough to believe he was actually communicating with Howard. On Thursday, the arrangements had been made and Garrett boarded his private plane for Grand Prairie, Texas with a revolver in his briefcase.

That same day, an unaware Howard received a message at his hotel in Mexico. *Howard, you're too obvious. If I was able to find you, so can the law. I have documents that will get you overseas. I have cash for you also. I will be at the Beacon Hotel Grand Prairie, Texas on Friday at nine am. Wait for me outside. Iron man.*

After Garrett arrived at the hotel on Thursday afternoon, he deposited his bag in his room and went down to the dining room for a leisurely dinner. He returned to his room, showered and propped himself up in bed with a glass of brandy.

In the morning, Garrett pulled his rented car to the front of the hotel and slowly circled the drive. He spotted someone standing by the front gate, partially hidden by the bushes. He slowed and looked more carefully at the man. He was unshaven with a wrinkled jacket pulled close to his body. When Garrett passed him the second time, he stopped. The man slowly walked toward the car and bent down to look inside. "It's about time," he said. He opened the door and slid in next to Garrett.

"You look terrible and you smell. How long has it been since you took a shower?" Garrett said.

"That's none of your damn business. Lets just get out of here. Why did you pick this place? Sure was far enough out of town." They were silent until the city was fading away and the long dusty roads of Texas lay before them.

"So, how did you find me, Garrett?" Howard asked.

"What do you mean, how did I find you? You were the one who contacted me, that's how I found you," Garrett answered.

Howard sat up straight in the seat. "Is this a setup? Are you turning me in?" His head jerked around looking to see if they were being followed.

Garrett pulled the car over to the side of the deserted road. "I'm not buying this. I know you needed money and I was just waiting to hear from you. You didn't do your job, Howard. You messed it all up. How am I supposed to trust someone who can't do a simple little thing for me and then disappears?" He reached into his pocket and pulled out a revolver. "Get out of the car, Howard."

"Hold on, Garrett. Let's talk about this. You're making a big mistake. I got rid of Ari just like you told me. I just needed a little vacation. I had a broken nose. Just let me walk away. I'll keep my mouth shut, I promise. I think someone is setting us up."

"You're an ass, Howard. The police questioned me for hours after they found Ari's body. You screwed it up royally. Why should I let you live to screw something else up for me? I said, get out of the car!"

Howard slowly opened the door. "Come on, now. This ain't necessary. Come on, Garrett. I done good for you. Just let me walk away," he said in a shaky voice. Knowing this was his last chance to make a run for it, Howard ducked behind the door and then bolted forward. He ran across the open field as fast as his heavy legs would carry him. He stumbled several times and began gasping for his breath. Turning around he realized that Garrett was not following him, so he slowed down.

Garrett slowly exited the car and watched as Howard tried to move his cumbersome body across the rutted field. Garrett smiled. *It was almost like hunting big game. You gave them a chance to get away, and then you go after them.* Howard would be an easy target. Garrett sauntered into the field with the gun at his side. He knew that he could out run Howard without breaking a sweat. Howard was now in his sight.

He was completely out of breath, a wheezing sound and sobs escaped from his throat as he tried to climb a small dune.

"Howard," Garrett called out. Howard stopped. He dropped to his knees and put his hands over his head. He did not turn around. "Please don't kill me, Garrett. Please." Two shots rang out and Howard fell face forward into the dirt. With adrenalin coursing through his veins, Garrett walked up the slope and stood over him. He watched as the blood seeped from the holes in his jacket. Garrett nudged Howard's body with his foot. Watching the last few minutes of life, he pointed the gun at the back of Howard's head and squeezed the trigger one more time. Howard would be buzzard food before Garrett ate his next meal.

Two days later in Los Angeles the telephone rang in Michael's house. He answered it on the second ring. "Howard's dead. Some bikers found his body in a field. He was shot three times, once at close range. You haven't been in Texas, have you Michael?"

"Nope. Haven't left LA. Thanks Taylor. You made my day."

"I got a good idea who did this one. It's time to step up your plan, Michael. Are you ready?" Taylor said.

"Yes, I am," he replied. Soon the noose would be tightening around Garrett's neck ever so slowly cutting off the air that kept him alive. "Are you sure the plan is going to work?"

"Let's hope so," Taylor replied. "I'll see you in the morning."

Taylor sat in Michael's office. "Here is the plan I have lined out. It should take care of Garrett Ferrell."

Michael leaned back in the chair and read the paper. "Wow, this is pretty radical, Taylor."

"I know, but I've given it a lot of thought." Taylor replied. "I'm going to take it slow just like you wanted. Time is on our side right now."

"We never talk much, Taylor. I have a question I've been dying to ask you. Are you doing this just for the money or do you have another agenda for helping me out? You never have told me what happened between you and Garrett."

Taylor was silent for a moment. "The money is good, Michael. Don't get me wrong, I love the money, but I also love a challenge. Believe me this is one hell of a challenge. Besides I like to see the good guys in white hats win." He changed the subject. "Now, are you clear about all the items you need to bring back from Carol? It's real important that you try to get everything on the list."

Michael nodded.

"See you in a couple of days." He didn't answer Michael's question.

The leader of the Lambingo tribe in Malawi called a meeting of the chieftains from several neighboring tribes. The elephant with the white spot on his ear was causing a great deal of damage in their fields of corn and wheat that bordered the thick brush. They had seen him several times tramping through the rows of vegetation leaving nothing behind but crippled plants. It was time to make him leave the area. They would not kill him unless he challenged them. They would communicate with each other to make sure they were aware of his whereabouts and find ways to chase him off.

The villagers began firing their guns in the air whenever Jakuta was sighted near the fields. It did not take long for him to get the message and return to roaming the Savannah.

Chapter Twenty-Six

Michael rented a car at the airport in Rome and drove into the city. He found an open jewelry store and bought his mother a gold cross on a thin chain. After it was wrapped he left the store and headed to the convent. The car that was trailing him veered off just before reaching the gate. The driver was satisfied that Michael was indeed going to see his mother.

Walking into the garden, Michael was surprised at what he saw—two women, both in blue dresses, covered by brown aprons, snipping roses from a bush. They were talking and laughing.

"Mom," he called out.

Rosa turned, wiping her hands on her apron. "Michael! My goodness what are you doing here?" She crossed the short distance between them and put her arms around his neck. She kissed his cheek. "I'm so happy to see you."

Michael looked over his shoulder, the other woman smiled at him. It was Carol Grey. *He had told her to stay away from his mother. What was she doing?*

"You know Carol, don't you Michael?"

"Yes," he replied sternly.

Rosa took his arm. "Carol and I have become good friends. She loves flowers as much as I do. And oh, she has helped me so much with my depression. I do believe I am ready to forgive Frank for what he did. I still miss him terribly, but life does go on."

Carol walked behind them not saying a word. Occasionally, Michael would glance over his shoulder at her.

That evening he had dinner with his mother on the terrace of the convent. He gave her the cross. She touched it with her fingers and tears ran down her cheeks. He helped her put it around her neck. "Are you ready to leave here, Mom?" he asked.

"Soon, I think I'll be ready soon. I want to do some traveling while I'm here in Italy. I hope that will be all right with you. Carol said she would go with me if I wanted a traveling companion. What do you think of that idea, Michael?"

He wanted to tell her that it was a bad idea. How could he have his mother traveling with the woman who stood by while others died? Besides Carol Grey's time at the convent was coming to an end. "We'll talk about that later, Mom. I need to go to the hotel. Jet lag is catching up with me. I'll see you in the morning."

Before leaving, Michael went to the reception room of the convent and asked the Sister on duty if she would please call Miss Grey's room and tell her she had a visitor in the lobby. He paced the floor until he saw her coming down the stairs. "We need to talk," he said.

"I know you're upset with me, Michael. I know I should have stayed away from your mother but I felt so sorry for her. I hate to see her suffer. She is a wonderful woman and I would never do anything to hurt her."

"You already have, Carol." He took her arm and lightly pulled her into the chapel across the hall. "Now, I have a plan that I need your help with. Ari and Howard are both dead. Howard killed Ari and I am positive that Garrett had Howard killed. Who knows maybe he was even stupid enough to do it himself. Either way, Garrett is my next target."

"I'm glad they're both dead. I hated those evil men. They deserved what they got. I've been working long hours on getting all the information transcribed from the papers you gave me. I've been able to link to almost every site in Garrett's computer. I know the names of all his illegal associates and how much each one has invested in Garrett's company. The information is yours whenever you want it."

"Taylor thinks it is time for you to come back to the states. So is Carol Grey ready to die?" Michael asked.

Her eyes widened. "Have you come here to kill me?"

"No, you are going to be reinvented. Carol Grey is going to die. She is going to be found dead. I don't have all the details yet. Taylor is taking care of all the arrangements." Carol's mouth dropped open.

"I want to take it slow. I don't want the authorities to get in on this until I am sure that Garrett doesn't have another grand scheme to prove himself innocent. We have got to make this work. You will have to stay here until I am sure that Garrett knows about your death. He'll have it all checked out, but this time we have the upper hand. When I get the all clear I'll let you know." Michael reached into his pocket and pulled out a sheet of paper. "Now, this is the stuff I have to take back with me." He handed the paper to Carol.

"My goodness, this is just about everything I have with me. If I give you my passport how am I ever going to leave Europe?"

"You start thinking about who you would like to be. Maybe one of the sister's here has an old, expired passport that you can alter. You're good at that. I want you to prepare my mother for your departure so that she is not upset about you leaving. I don't want her back in the states until everything is settled." As he rose to leave, his voice softened. "I suppose I should be grateful for you helping my mother. She seems a lot happier than the last time I saw her. I'll stop by tomorrow for the things."

Michael spent the next day with his mother and then left Rome for the states with Carol's luggage with him.

Taylor looked through the suitcase lying open on the desk. "You did good, Michael. This is everything I need. I'm going to leave for a couple of days. I have to go kill Carol Grey. I'm going to fly to New York and then rent a car. If you need me, just call my cell phone. The next step is all up to me. You just sit tight in L.A. and make some more money."

Taylor took the luggage and went back to his hotel. Sitting on the side of the bathtub he dumped the suitcase, the purse and the papers into the filled tub. He threw in two of the potted plants from the room making a pool of muddy water before he pulled the plug on the drain. He put the soggy mess on the windowsill to dry. He then put it all into a plastic bag and tied it shut. In a few days it will appear as if the contents of the bag had been in water for quite a while.

The trails cut through the Savannah were not marked. There was nothing to guide the thousands of animals across the open plains except their instincts. The same paths had been traveled for hundred of years. The destination was always the same, the search for food and water to give them strength enough to produce the next generation of their kind.

Chapter Twenty-Seven

Taylor's destination was a small town near the Canadian border called Houlton, Maine. It was the last American town before you crossed the border. It had been over ten years since he had been in Houlton, but to him it looked exactly the same. His life had changed, but Houlton had not. Driving down the main street everything seemed familiar to Taylor. He had spent three long months in the Madison Hotel just off Oak Street during a very cold winter. Today it was sunny and warm and the street was busy with tourists. Driving slowly, Taylor found his destination and turned into the parking lot. He got out and walked up the steps of the Houlton Police Department. The clerk at the desk directed him down the hallway to the office of the Chief of Police, Lawrence Becker. Opening the door, Taylor asked, "Anybody home?"

A grin covered Larry's face as he got up from his desk and bounded across the floor. "Taylor Rhinehart, you old son of a gun. My gosh, it's good to see you. What in the hell are you doing in these parts?"

They made idle conversation for a few minutes before Taylor said, "I wish I could say I'm here on a pleasure trip, but actually, it's business. What time you get off duty? I'd like to buy you dinner."

"I got a better idea. You come on over to the house around five and Becky will fix you a home cooked meal. How does that sound?" Larry asked.

"Sounds good to me. Is the Madison Hotel still open for business?"

"Sure is, but now it's a bed and breakfast. I'll meet you here at five and we can ride out to the house together." He gave Taylor's hand a hardy shake.

Taylor checked into the Madison and unpacked a few of his clothes and hung them in the closet. He took the bag holding Carol's possessions and put it under the bed.

Lying across the bed, he closed his eyes. The memories of his time in Houlton came flooding into his mind.

He remembered the first tear-filled telephone call from Larry. Taylor was in his investigation office in New York, when the call came through. Larry was beset with grief. His fifteen-year-old son had been accused of rape by one of his classmates after she suffered a painful miscarriage. Taylor remembered his own irritation, wondering why this small town cop would be calling him. The man said he was Jeannie's older brother. He desperately needed help. Every plea for his son had been exhausted and the boy still proclaimed his innocence. It was his love for Jeannie that made Taylor decide to look into the matter. That's how he ended up in Houlton for over three months. By the end of three months he had collected all the evidence he needed to finally make the girl confess that it was indeed her own father who was abusing her and had threatened to kill her if she told anyone. On his last day in Houlton, when his son was set free, Larry told Taylor if he ever needed a favor, come to him. So here he was. Getting ready to ask a huge favor.

After a wonderful dinner of chicken and dumplings, Larry and Taylor sat on the front porch drinking their coffee.

"So are you going to tell me why you're here?" Larry asked. "I've invited you here before and you were always too busy. So what is going on now that brought you to Houlton?"

"I'm here to ask a favor. I hate to involve you in all this, but without your help I may not succeed in what I am trying to accomplish. I have a client that has got caught up in the middle of something that is bigger than he can handle. So big, in fact, he has no idea that if he doesn't do everything just right there is going to be a lot of people looking for him. And when they find him he'll be a dead man. He wants to vindicate his father, who was killed because he knew too much."

Larry leaned his chair against the wall. "You've lost me, Taylor. I haven't got a clue what you're talking about."

"Well let me ask you this, Larry. Do you have any unclaimed bodies laying around the morgue right now that have no destination?"

"Whoa, hold on. You need a body?'

"Yes, I need a totally decomposed body that looks like its been in water for about seven months. Know where I can get one?"

"All I got is a body that was found in the quarry about a year ago, when we were looking for some stolen cars. We pulled the corpse out and it has never been identified. It's still in the freezer at the morgue."

"Man or woman?" Taylor asked.

"Man."

"Well, that might work, depends on what we do with it. Now I'm going to start at the beginning of the story." And he did. He told Larry all about Garrett Ferrell and his money laundering business. He told him about all the innocent people Ferrell had killed and why it was important to get Carol back to the states so she could help Michael deplete all the funds from Garrett's accounts and then hopefully have him arrested.

"You see, Larry, without Carol's help, it's Michael's word against Garrett, even though Michael has the papers. Garrett can still level charges against Michael's father. And also, if Michael releases the papers he will probably have some unsavory characters after him. People he really doesn't want to mess with. The ones that Ferrell left holding the bag."

"Okay, I got the story, but where does the body come in?" Larry said, in a puzzled voice.

"I want Garrett to think that Carol was on her way to Canada when her car went off the road and she ended up in Deer River. You just happened to find the car and body within the last couple of weeks. I'll have someone on the New York Times put a small paragraph in the back page of the paper, but I think that Garrett will probably send somebody here to check it all out. I have the water soaked luggage, Carol's purse and all her papers. That should be proof enough, but…if they want to see a body, I have to produce one. How far off base am I?"

"It's just crazy enough to work. So all I have to do is unfreeze my old corpse, and keep the luggage and purse here. Is that right? Is that all I have to do?"

"Yes," Taylor answered.

"Piece of cake. I'll be glad to do it for you, Taylor."

Taylor let out a sigh of relief. Carol Grey would soon be deceased.

The next morning with the plan all in place, Taylor prepared to leave Houlton. Standing by the car, he waved goodbye to Becky. "Here, I want to give you this," he said handing Larry an envelope. "It's for you and your wife. Go take a long vacation in Hawaii or go see your son and his family in Texas. You deserve it. You're a good man."

He got into his car and drove away before Larry opened the envelope and found the check for twenty-five thousand dollars.

On the long trip from Houlton Taylor had a lot of time to think. He popped the top on a can of Coke and turned on the radio. Punching the buttons he smiled when all he could find was county music. He remembered how Jeannie loved country music. They argued about it all the time when the radio was on in the car, but he always let her win. Wouldn't she be surprised to know that he had been given a second chance to get even with Garrett Ferrell? God, how he hated that man. He had ruined his life and now Taylor was going to make sure he did the same and even more to him. He had taken away the only job he ever loved and the only woman he loved more. So many years ago, such clear memories.

He and Jeannie had been sweethearts since college. When Taylor decided to leave the Midwest to join the New York Police Force, instead of going back to her home in Maine, Jeannie moved right along with him. She hated the big city, but if that was what Taylor wanted she would be right there with him.

They rented an apartment and she got a job working in the mailroom at Ferrell Enterprises. They ate pizza on the floor of their apartment and made love on the small balcony at night. She worried about him when he graduated and started patrolling the streets, but he convinced her that everything would be all right.

They planned to marry but never seemed to get around to it. After two years when Jeannie was promoted to the secretarial pool, and he got a promotion to sergeant they started looking around for a better place to live. They moved to the lower east side of New York. Once again, she knew no one.

And then everything seemed to change. He was working late almost every night, falling into bed just a few hours before she got up to go to work. They seldom saw each other. He stopped paying attention to her and became totally engrained in the New York crime scene. She was lonely and scared living in the big city, especially after listening to the stories that Taylor would relate to her. As the days dwindled by she began to slip away from him and he was too engrossed in his own life to notice. And then it happened. Jeannie was promoted to Houston Ferrell's reception office and she met Houston's son, Garrett. She was a novelty to Garrett. He was good looking, suave and a hunter of unsuspecting victims— like a small town girl named Jeannie. He made fun of her accent and it made her giggle. He took her to lunch and put vases of yellow roses on her desk. She was swept off her feet by all his glib lies. And when she finally thought she was madly in love with Garrett, she told Taylor she was leaving him. He was stunned and he begged her to stay. She moved into her own tiny apartment leaving Taylor to spend lonely hours without her, realizing what a terrible mistake he had made.

Garrett lost interest in her in less than three months. When he said he didn't want to see her anymore she begged him to take her back until he became so irritated he had her fired.

A week later Taylor got a call that Jeannie had taken an overdose of drugs. Her landlady found her after smelling a foul odor coming from Jeannie's apartment. The autopsy confirmed that she was about four weeks pregnant when she died. She left a note for Taylor telling him how sorry she was for what she had done and she was sure he would never forgive her.

Taylor should have hated her for leaving him, but as much as he tried, he still loved her. It was his fault. He would have taken her back in a heartbeat even after what she had done to him. Her death hit him hard. One of the officer's on the force that questioned Garrett said he called Jeannie a stupid bimbo and had no idea why she would even believe that he loved her.

Five years later when Taylor was promoted to detective, Garrett Ferrell came under his scrutiny. The case he was assigned to involved a drug lord named Alphonse who agreed to testify against Garrett in exchange for immunity. He knew more than he should and Taylor knew the information would be enough to convict Garrett on money laundering charges. Taylor tried to keep Alphonse under wraps but Garrett found him and Alphonse disappeared. Garrett was furious about the investigation. He paid off a few people and Taylor was put before the police board accused of planting drugs in Garrett's company. With no proof that Alphonse even existed, Taylor was fired from the police department.

With his own investigation company in San Francisco up and running, Taylor thought that at some point in his life he would be able to go after Garrett again. Taylor didn't have enough time or money to satisfy his hate for him. It would have to wait. And now the time had come.

When it came to dominance in the elephant world there were no boundaries— father against son, brother against brother. The weak will yield to the strong.

Chapter Twenty-Eight

Garrett sat at the bar at the country club. He glanced at his watch. Elliott was late as usual. They had an eleven o'clock tee time. It was eleven-twenty. He nodded to the bartender who came forward and refilled Garrett's glass. It was early to be drinking, but he didn't care.

His son interrupted Garrett's thoughts, "Sorry, I'm late. We'd better get on the tee, Dad." Elliott was well aware of his father's displeasure with him.

Garrett was silent until they reached the first tee. Stepping out of the golf cart, he asked, "How was your trip to California? And Michael, how is he doing?"

"The trip was okay. Michael is hanging out with Shay Young. Kind of pisses me off. He knows that she and I were dating at one time. Shay is living in California so I guess it doesn't matter anyway. I don't plan on moving to the West Coast."

Garrett sensed it was time to put the rift between Elliott and Michael. He could tell that Elliott was already unsettled about Shay. It might be a good time to make him dislike Michael even more.

Garrett had been monitoring Michael's every move for the last eight months and he had never given Garrett one clue that he had the papers or the money. Yet, Garrett could not rule out that Michael was just biding his time and waiting for the perfect moment to strike. "I have something to tell you, Elliott. I never said anything before, but sometimes I find it hard to deal with your friendship with Michael after what his father did to me."

"What are you talking about? What did Mr. Charpelli do to you?"

"I know this is going to be hard for you to believe, but for years, Frank was skimming money from the company. He was a pretty clever man and found a way to set up an account for himself without anyone knowing about it. He took millions of dollars from my company. He had access to huge sums of money on a daily basis and I suppose he knew how to take advantage of it. I can tell by the look on your face, Elliott that you're surprised. That's not the only thing Frank did to me. He also found a way to get into the files of all our clients. I'm sure he was planning on selling the information to my competitors. He would have ruined me, Elliott. Luckily I found out about all of it. When I faced him with the evidence and the fact that he would probably spend the rest of his life in prison it must have been too much for him. So, he killed himself."

Elliott was speechless. "I can't believe any of this. Frank Charpelli was a wonderful man. I've known him ever since I was a kid. Why would he do such a thing? He made good money."

"Greed, Elliott, just pure greed. Even though I have never found the account with the money in it or the documents he had, I still couldn't bring myself to tell the authorities. I knew you had a close relationship with Michael and I didn't want to make it any worse for him or Mrs. Chapelli."

Elliott was livid. "That's even harder for me to believe. When did you get morals all of a sudden? You're telling me that you let him get away with your money and documents that could ruin your company and you were concerned about Michael's mother or our friendship? You were the one who just got done trying to frame your own wife to save money, so I think your story is all bullshit, Dad. What's the real story?"

Garrett glared at his son. "It's my whole life's work, Elliott and if it goes down the drain, so will you. Everything will be gone. Do you think you would enjoy being poor? I have a feeling that Michael may know where those documents are and he is keeping it a secret."

Elliott tossed his golf club over his head. "I'm done." He started walking toward the clubhouse.

Elliott slid into his car and threw his golf glove on the seat. His eyes rested on the glove compartment. It was coming back to him. The night of Frank's funeral Mrs. Charpelli had given him a brown envelope. He put it in the car. Opening the glove box, he stared inside. It wasn't there. Elliott beat on the steering wheel with his fists. No, no, there was no way that what his father told him was true. He would go to L.A. and find out for himself.

Stepping out of the car, he waited until his father pulled the golf cart to a stop next to the clubhouse. "How much money did Frank take?"

"Over twenty seven million dollars of my, or I mean… our money."

"I'm going to L.A. tonight. If this is all true, I'm going to beat the crap out of Michael Charpelli. You better believe I'll get our money back."

"I'm warning you, Elliott, you have to handle this carefully. If Michael has no idea what you are talking about he will probably be more surprised than you were. But, if he was aware of what his father was doing he'll probably have some sort of story already made up about me—something crazy, like I killed his father. Trust me, he's going to try and convince you that I'm some kind of monster and he deserved the money. As far as the papers are concerned I have no idea what value they would be to him unless he has already found a buyer for them. Be careful. Don't be too vulnerable when you face him. I'll call my pilot and have the plane ready for you whenever you want to leave."

Jakuta entered the ring of bulls that seemed to be in a state of frenzy. Several young cows had broken away from the herd and joined the males. It was a most unusual situation. The young bulls sensed that they might have a chance to mate even though three larger males had entered the arena. Waiting for an opening a young male charged after a female who was receptive to his advances. Within a few feet of her Jakuta intercepted him. He had waited. It had become an interesting game to him. Frustrated the younger bull let out a loud bellow and yielded. He had no choice.

Chapter Twenty-Nine

When Michael returned home from Rome he was surprised to find Elliott was back in Los Angeles and staying at his house. He found him sitting on his patio with a bottle of Chavez next to him. Elliott seemed disconnected, answering Michael's questions in short, curt sentences. His reply as to why he was there was that he had simply gotten bored in New York.

Michael poured himself a drink and sat down. Elliott stared into the pool, sipping on his drink.

"When did you get here?" Michael asked.

"Yesterday. How come you never told me that you and Shay were living together?"

"The subject never came up," Michael answered.

"Bullshit! You were keeping it from me, weren't you? It doesn't matter anyway. I'll save that subject for another day. I'm here on a mission from my father. You got any idea what it's about?"

Michael's jaw tightened. He was caught off-guard. So, Garrett had finally pulled Elliott into his grasp.

"I know all about what happened with your father and the money. I know about the papers, too. I had them in my car. You took them didn't you?" The anger was creeping into Elliott's voice.

Michael knew it was time to give an academy award performance. "What papers? What money?"

"You know damn well what I'm talking about. Your father scammed twenty seven million dollars from my father and some information he had no right to. When my father found out about it, your dad knew he would go to jail so he hung himself."

Michael lunged at him, grabbing him by the front of his shirt. "You bastard. How can you say something like that about my dad? He was an honest man. If he stole from your father, prove it!" Michael shouted, angrily.

Elliott pulled away. He was shocked. "So, you're telling me that you had no idea about the money or the papers?

"I'm saying prove it. You're the one standing there telling me all this bullshit. I want proof. Who told you all this crap?"

"Your mother gave me an envelope the day after your father died. I put it in my car. Did you take it, Michael?"

"I have no idea what you're talking about. I never took anything from your car. Was I the only one who drove it other than you?"

"No, but who else would want those papers?" He hesitated for a minute. "You're serious. You didn't take the envelope and you don't know anything about the money."

"My father was a kind and decent man who went through some bad times and decided to take the chicken way out, but he wasn't a thief or a liar. Do you think if he left me all that money I would be out here busting my ass to start this company? Get out, Elliott. Get out of my house." *He had to keep going. He had to be convincing.*

"Wait just a minute, Michael, hear me out. I don't know why I even thought for a moment that my father was telling me the truth. He doesn't know anything about our trust in each other. I'm sorry I was stupid enough to believe him." Elliott poured another shot of Chavez and paced back and forth across the patio. "Remember when we were tethered together on Red Ridge Mountain and my clip slipped out of the wall. You risked your life to pull me up. You could have very easily unhooked the line to save yourself but you didn't. We had a close call when our kayak turned over in the Cheyenne River. But I managed to right it and saved our lives. You have to remember that we have a bond between us that will be there until we die and I think you know I just made one of the dumbest mistakes in my life." Elliott lowered his head. "What can I do to make you understand how sorry I am. Just give me one more chance. Damn it, Michael we've been friends too long. Don't forget that no matter what happens to us, at one time we were on top of the mountain."

He had punished Elliott enough for one day. "I'm really sick of it all, Elliott. Your father needs to get over what ever it is that's bothering him and quit trying to blame all his problems on someone else. I have enough of my own to get tangled up in another mess." *His performance was complete. He had put a wedge between himself and Elliott. Their bond of friendship was over.*

"I have to go into town and get some work done," Michael said. "Are you staying for a while?" He needed to get out of the house.

"I'll be leaving pretty soon, Michael. Are you sure we're okay?"

"Yeah, Elliott, everything is just fine. I'll see you in the morning."

Michael drove down the highway much too fast, taking the curves at fifty miles per hour. He needed to clear his head. Maybe he was becoming greedy. He should have just admitted he had the money and given it to Elliott with the promise that Elliott wouldn't tell Garrett he had it. Elliott was his best friend. Why was he so unsure that Elliott would go for that idea? If he gave him the money, he wouldn't have to worry how Elliott would fare once the Ferrell Group was destroyed. Yet…maybe he would just keep the money, even though his own mortgage company was doing well. A little cushion of twenty-seven million dollars wasn't a bad idea.

He stopped by his office, shuffling through a stack of papers on his desk. He got absolutely nothing done.

After eating dinner in a small, Italian restaurant he had several drinks at a nearby bar. Finding himself in no shape to drive all the way back home, he drove back to his office and crashed on the couch. He woke up around four a.m. with a pounding headache. It was time to go home. He wanted to see Shay.

The house was dark. He quietly went upstairs to the bedroom. A glimmer of light shone from beneath the bathroom door. 'Shay," he said softly. There was no answer. He called again.

"Come in," she said. Shay stood at the mirror in a white robe with a face full of cleansing cream.

"When did you get home?" he asked.

"Around midnight."

"Elliott was here earlier. Did he decide to stay the night?" Michael asked.

"No. He left right after I got home," she answered.

Michael put his arms around her waist. "What are you still doing up? You should be exhausted." He nuzzled her neck. "I love you," he whispered.

"I was worried about you. I wish you would have called or come home. It's almost morning." She turned and went into the bedroom. I have an early appointment today. Don't bother to get up. I'll see you tonight." He didn't see the tears in her eyes.

A few hours later, Shay got dressed and went for her morning run. Michael watched from the bedroom window as she sprinted down the driveway. She looked beautiful in her white shorts and tee shirt, her hair blowing in the morning breeze. Downstairs, he poured himself a second cup of coffee and sat down on the patio to wait for her. He knew something was bothering her. When he came to bed she pretended to be asleep. He could tell by her breathing that he had listened to so many nights. When he put his arm around her, she didn't move. She always had orange juice with him before her run. Today she left the house without talking to him. Something was wrong. He had an uneasy feeling.

After returning to the house, Shay went straight to the bedroom and undressed. She stepped into the shower and let the cool water run over her body. She dressed and bounded down the steps. She called to him. "I'm leaving. I have a hair appointment and I want to go shopping. I'll see you later."

Michael rattled around the house all day. A nagging feeling that something was wrong with Shay kept creeping into his mind. He made a few business calls and leafed through a weeks worth of mail. He decided to go to the gym and make a feeble attempt at a workout, but gave up after half an hour. He called Shay's cell phone several time only to reach her voice mail. Her car was in the driveway when he got home.

Michael leaned on the bathroom door watching her brush her hair. "What's wrong?" he asked.

"Nothing," she replied.

He put his hand on her shoulder. She turned away.

"Did you sleep with him?" Michael blurted out.

She didn't answer right away. " Why are you asking me that? What do you think, Michael?"

"I'm hoping that you didn't."

"Well then, you're thinking wrong." She threw the brush at him, barely missing his head. "You bastard! You left us here alone on purpose. Why, Michael, why? What kind of game are you playing?"

"You tell me, Shay. You tell me if it's a game. I thought we were a couple. I thought I could trust you. I was wrong."

"Then why did you set me up? Even if I told you what happened you wouldn't believe me."

"Try me," he answered.

She sat down on the side of the bed. "Everything was fine. He seemed in a good mood when I got home. He was drinking wine. He offered me a glass and I took it. I only had two glasses and then I started feeling heady. I hadn't eaten anything since breakfast and the wine really hit me. He kept talking about old times. Erotic times we spent together. That's when I left the room. I was so proud of myself. I took a long bath and went to bed. Everything would have been okay except I woke up about an hour later with a bad case of indigestion. I went downstairs to get a glass of milk. He was still on the balcony. He said there was a wonderful meteor shower going on. He rolled a couple of joints and I just took a couple of hits. Elliott started kissing me and telling me how much he had missed me and that he wished he had never let me go. My legs were getting wobbly. I remember he picked me up and carried me to my room. He was on top of me, pulling my robe off. He kept saying over and over that you didn't love me. You just wanted to see if you could take me away from him. He said it was all a game. I think I just passed out or something, but I can't remember much about being with him." She began to cry. "It had been so long since I've drank wine or smoked weed. I know it's no excuse. I'm sorry, Michael. I wish I could snap my fingers and say it never happened, but it did and you're right. You can't trust me. And you sure can't trust your friend." She pushed past him and went back into the bathroom. "I'll leave in the morning. I'm too tired right now."

"What if I told you I didn't want you to leave?" Michael asked.

"You'd better think about it. I'm tired. I need to sleep."

Michael lay on his side staring into the darkness. *God damn you, Elliott Ferrell. Why couldn't you leave her alone? There was now another hole in his heart caused by someone named Ferrell. I'm going to get even with you this time for sure.*

"Michael," she whispered. "Are you sleeping?"

He never answered her.

In the morning she was gone. She left a short note. *I am so sorry I hurt you. You deserve better. I am on my way to Jamaica for a few days. Shay*

He roamed around his house for days not even bothering to get dressed. He packed up the articles of her clothing he found in his bedroom and put all her cosmetics in a bag. He could still smell her on his tee shirts that she loved to wear to bed. He missed her, he ached for her. He still never called her.

Michael decided to email Taylor and tell him to call off the rest of the plan. He didn't care anymore about Garrett Ferrell. Michael wanted Shay.

The answer to his email was two words, *Too Late.*

Something had brought him to this place. A place he usually avoided. His senses had always told him that the road is where the trucks stopped and the hunters got out and hid behind the canvas tarps waiting to kill. Today he picked up a scent, a slight smell of a dead elephant.

Chapter Thirty

Harold McCabe placed the folded newspaper in front of Garrett. He tapped his finger on a three-paragraph article. "Look at this," he said. "Carol Grey is dead. Months looking for her and she's been dead all along."

Garrett grabbed the paper.

Houlton Times, Houlton, Maine

While searching for a stolen car in Deere Lake the police have found a vehicle at the bottom of the lake. On further inspection the body of a woman was found inside the car. It appears that she has been dead for at least three months. There is no evidence of foul play. Ruts running down the bank indicate the automobile skidded off the road. The body has been identified as one, Carol Grey— a resident of New York City and former employee of Ferrell Enterprises. The police department has been unable to locate the next of kin and is holding the body until such time that it is claimed.

"Go up there and check this out. Go today! I am not buying this story until I'm sure it's Carol." Garrett had nothing more to say.

Detective McCabe's visit to Houlton's Police Department was met with complete cooperation. He was shown the muddy suitcase and its contents and also Carol's purse. McCabe looked through the purse, pulling out the passport, her driver's license, three thousand dollars in cash, and a brown envelope filled with muddy, ink-smeared writing. Removing his rubber gloves he put everything back in the evidence basket and pushed it across the counter.

"Now, Detective McCabe would you like to see the body? There isn't much left—just a skeleton with a few strands of hair left on her head. That long in the water really decomposes a body fast, but of course you know all that. Anyway I got dental records. You want them?" Larry said, hoping that McCabe had seen enough.

"No, that's okay. You just hold on to it, okay."

Larry sucked in his breath. "Sure thing. You need anything else, let us know."

McCabe turned and left. Larry let out a sigh of relief.

Garrett's reaction to the news that Carol was dead and the papers were ruined came as one of disbelief. If it was true, he could get back to business. He asked McCabe over and over if he felt the information was true. McCabe agreed to investigate the incident further, but didn't see much point in it. Carol was probably on her way to Canada, crossing the seldom-used back roads to keep undercover. Who knows, it may have been raining or dark, or even both that caused her car to go off the road.

Taking the five thousand dollars from Garrett, McCabe stuck the money in his coat pocket and returned to Houlton one more time. The information he got was the same and he saw no reason why the police chief would lie to him. As far as he was concerned Carol Grey was dead. But where was the twenty-seven million dollars?

Within a month illegal foreign currency was once again flowing into Ferrell Enterprises from several Asian countries. Garrett's new staff had been plied with money and were taking on tasks that they had no idea were illegal. Just like all those before them they were pawns in Garrett's scheme. Garrett felt smug and invincible. He was totally unaware that a few blocks away, Peggy Bowling, aka Carol Grey, was living in an upscale hotel. Spending most of her daylight hours at her computer, the new Peggy continued to finalize the information Frank had written down into credible information. She now had the names, account numbers and banks where Garrett was depositing his ill-gotten gains.

In order to buy her a few more days, she and Taylor spent time together creating diversions to keep Garrett off his game. A gas leak in one of Garrett's major warehouses closed down the facility for several days. The port authorities were also looking into a complaint about improper shipping lanes at the four docks that Garrett's importing division used. A bomb threat at the Ferrell building caused the entire building to be evacuated for an entire afternoon. Garrett was irritated and angry at the recent events, screaming at his personnel to get things fixed and quickly. It was taking away time that he would normally spend creating more dummy accounts. Taylor was amused at the idea that the money Michael was supplying to him could buy such favors.

How could an elephant ever know that the tusks that he carried were more valuable than his life? How could he ever know that he could be killed just for those two long ivory tusks that help protect him from his enemies and sometime cause him a great deal of trouble when they became tangled in the thick vines that covered the trees? He would never know, until it was too late.

Chapter Thirty-One

Carol Grey looked out her window from her suite in the Armbruster Hotel. She loved New York and the view from the hotel was stunning except for one black spot on the horizon. The Ferrell Building—the towering edifice two streets from her hotel glowed an eerie green at night. Garrett had installed the emerald green lights on the top floors. He said it made his building stand out from the other buildings.

That building was her first prison, the brownstone where she lived became her second, the convent in Rome became her third and now the suite in the Armbruster was her new cell. She wondered if she would ever be free to walk the streets of New York, take in a Broadway show or even eat in an obscure restaurant without being watched or followed or worried someone would find her. The ringing of the telephone interrupted her thoughts. She told the desk clerk that it was all right for Taylor to come up to her room.

After a few minutes of small talk, with Carol telling Taylor she remembered his name from years ago and Taylor thanking her for recommending him to Michael, Carol offered him a drink. Sensing he wanted to get right down to business, Carol showed him to her computer desk. He pulled up a chair and sat down next to her.

"Okay, let me explain how this works," she said, pointing to the screen. "It has taken me months to put this together from the papers Michael gave me. Frank wasn't aware of how the system worked so many of his notes were in random order. They were difficult to decipher."

She pointed to the screen. "In this first column are the legal accounts handled at Ferrell. As you can see they make a tidy profit, but of course not enough for him. In the second column are the accounts that are illegal. Right now there are six. Garrett had a lot more before Frank died. These six are all foreign companies. The first three sold arms and ammunition, two are bringing illegal substances into the country and one is just a very bad government official skimming money from his country. As you can see there is a lot of activity going on. All are dangerous men that we really need to stay away from. Here is the interesting column," Carol said, tapping the screen. "This is where Garrett hides the money he cleans up—his personal fortune. This is where we can hit him hard. With very little effort I can take the money out of these accounts and transfer it anywhere we want it to go."

"Amazing," Taylor remarked. "Now I can see why Garrett wanted those papers and also why he wanted you dead, Peggy."

Carol screwed up her face. "I hate the name Peggy. Anyway, Michael has given me the name of several banks he wants the accounts in. I have no idea what he plans to do with it, but that is his problem. So let's get started."

The first account they chose contained four million dollars. It was put in the name of Andy Paxton, who was a janitor at Ferrell Enterprises. "Wouldn't Andy be shocked to know he had four million dollars in an Italian bank," Carol said. "So, sorry, Andy, it's all gone now." She had just finished her sentence when the flashing red prompt, *Account Closed*, appeared on the screen.

"Now, here is an interesting one," Carol said, "Janice Carpenter has been dead for over four years. She has three million dollars in her account."

"How long will it take Garrett to notice these accounts are closed?"

"I don't think he will know for a while. He has a lot on his mind right now. If you want to really throw him a curve we could transfer one of these accounts to the legal income. His accountants would go wild trying to figure out where it came from."

"Let's take care of another one of these first." Five million dollars from a clerk who worked in the filing department was closed out and put into the daily transfer file under miscellaneous income. She leaned back in her chair. "Tomorrow is going to be pure chaos in the accounting department." She let out a soft giggle. "That's enough for today, we mustn't get greedy."

Taylor stood up and stretched. "I'll take that drink now."

They sat on the terrace taking in the evening air. "So, once this is all over with, what are your plans?" Taylor asked. "I suppose it will just be nice not to look over your shoulder every minute."

"I have no idea. I'll have to wait and see how it all comes out. Hopefully, I can have some sort of life." She raised her glass. "Here's to a very happy ending."

He clinked his glass against hers. *She really wasn't a bad looking woman— sort of plain, but a pleasant face.* "You ever been married, Carol?" He had no idea why he asked that question. He just wanted enough conversation so he could finish his drink.

She shook her head. "No. It was always my plan to marry and I really wanted children, but Garrett took that dream away. How about you? Have you ever been married?"

"No." he answered, "There was someone I cared a lot about a long time ago, but she died." He stood up. "I better get going. It's getting late."

She could sense he didn't want to talk about it any further. She walked him to the door.

As he turned to leave, he hesitated for a minute. "Just to let you know, Carol, I probably hate Garrett Ferrell more than you. But that's a story for another night."

Carol made herself another drink and sat down in front of her computer. She smiled to herself. She wondered what would happen if she took about ten million dollars and gave it to one of the illegal accounts. What would they do when they saw that much money coming back at one time? Probably go ballistic. They would wonder what Garrett was up to. The cleaned-up money was supposed to be given to them only in increments of one million dollars at a time. Maybe she should dump it all in their laps. It was something to think about. She logged off the computer and closed the laptop.

She lay in bed, restless, tossing and turning. Random thoughts were running through her mind. Tonight was the first time she had sat and had a drink with someone that was halfway pleasant. It had been so long. She still missed Daniel. It would be nice to have a relationship with someone again. Why had she been so dishonest to herself and everyone else all these years? Honesty would have kept her out of this mess and Michael's father would still be alive. She had only told Michael half of the story. The other half was too painful for her even to think about, much less tell anyone.

She thought about the early days when she first started working in Houston's office. Every time Garrett would come into the office she felt her heart skip a beat, but he wasn't at all attracted to her. In fact, he completely ignored her. She tried wearing her hair in different styles; she bought new clothes and crammed her feet into killer high heels. Nothing seemed to work. She wasn't appealing to him. Yet there was something about him that made her want him even more. As time passed she tried to make herself as invaluable to him as she could. It would eventually lead to her downfall. If only she hadn't been so stupid, she would have had a much different life. Her thoughts wandered back to the early days.

She was the one that made sure Garrett found out about her affair with Daniel. She dropped subtle hints around the office and eventually it got back to Garrett. She wanted to prove to Garrett that she wasn't a prude. It worked. After working late one evening, he called her into his office on the pretense of asking her about an account. He sat on the edge of his desk smiling at her. He wanted to know all about her affair with Daniel. She was embarrassed, but she told him what she could force herself to say. When he blurted out the question "Is Daniel a good lover?", she stood up to leave. He blocked the door and before she could say anything he pulled her into his arms and kissed her. He kissed her over and over—long-wet kisses, his tongue playing inside her mouth. His hand traveled under her sweater and his fingers fondled her breast. He pressed his body against her and she could feel every inch of him. She was breathless thinking he was actually going to make love to her. She felt his hand go under her skirt and skip down into her panties. She let out a moan and unzipped his pants. And then suddenly he grabbed her hand and pushed it away. He zipped up his pants and dismissed her like a discarded pair of old shoes, telling her she could go. He left her standing there and went into the bathroom and shut the door. That was all he wanted. He wanted to know he could have her at any time. She was so ashamed and embarrassed. How could she have left herself fall prey to him like the other stream of women employees who made visits to his office? What was wrong with her? She was having an affair with a married man and at the same time trying to seduce her boss. Neither would come to a good end.

Carol sat up and slipped her feet into her slippers. She retrieved the bottle of wine from the refrigerator and held it up to the light. Pouring the remains into a water glass she went back to her computer. *What should she do? Michael saved her life and for that she was grateful. If Garrett would have found her she would be dead by now, but...Michael was dragging his feet. It was his relationship with Elliott that was keeping him from moving faster on destroying Garrett. He knew what it was going to do to his friend, but it had to be done. If he hesitated much longer Garrett would get away again. And for her and Michael it would never be over until Garrett was completely obliterated.*

Carol took a long drink of the wine. She had made her decision. It would only take about half an hour and Garrett would be on the hit list of everybody in column B. She wondered how he would feel when he was hunted down like one of the elephants he killed with no where to hide and no one to protect him? Maybe she would just kill him, but this might be more fun.

She logged back into Garrett's accounts. Creating a new spreadsheet she began to divide the accounts into two columns. "Let's see, one for Garrett, one for me, one for Garrett, one for me, one for Garrett…"

Large herds of animals were gathering on the Savannah. It was time for the migration. The drought was near. They had to move quickly before the water holes began to dry up. Many would die on the long trek and others would be born.

Chapter Thirty-Two

Garrett's maid rushed up the middle of the long staircase in a fit of panic. "Senor Garrett, Senor Garrett come quick. There are men, many men, outside. The phone, it will not stop ringing. You come quickly." She wrung her hands on her apron.

"What the hell are you yammering about?" Garrett opened the door and looked over the balcony. "What is it?"

"You look out window. You see," she said in her broken English.

"Jesus, what's going on?" News vehicles, and reporters occupied the complete front lawn. They stood three deep on the porch and steps.

Garrett picked up his cell phone and dialed his office. There was no answer. He called several numbers before he reached one of his employees. "Bogart, what is going on? I just got out of bed, my house is surrounded by news people."

"Turn on the television, Mr. Ferrell." Garrett crossed the room and flipped on the television. It took him only a few minutes to find out that his company had dumped over fifty million dollars worth of stock on the market and was also sending large sums of money to his overseas accounts. The same news was on every channel.

"I'll be at the office in twenty minutes. Have all the department heads in the board room," he said to Bogart.

"There are only six of us here. Some of the men came to work, but when they saw what was going on they turned around and left. We can't get out of the building. There is too much confusion."

"Stay put, I'm on my way. This is all a big mistake." Garrett hung up the phone and dialed his chauffeur's number. "Get the Hummer. Bring it around back by the pool house. I'll be waiting for you." He escaped from the house unnoticed.

Once inside the car, Garrett flipped open his lap top and typed in the code that would access his private accounts. Staring at him was a message that read, *Have a good day.* "Son of a bitch," he screamed and threw the computer on the floor.

Arriving at the Ferrell building, his driver pulled the car into the underground garage, trying to avoid the barrage of reporters that hovered around the entrance. With camera's flashing and questions being thrown at him, Garrett rushed into his private elevator. Once in his office, he grabbed the intercom speaker and yelled into it. "I want every corporate head on this floor in the conference room, now! Right now!"

Three men were seated by the time he arrived at the table. " Where are the rest of the staff?" he asked.

Silence fell over the room. "I said, where in the hell is the rest of my department heads?"

Someone in the back of the room cleared his throat. "They left, Mr. Ferrell. When the newsmen and cameras starting showing up most of them left very quickly."

"Just like rats leaving a sinking ship," he growled. "Well, I'll see to them later. We are in trouble. Big trouble. Someone has broken into our computer system and is dumping huge amounts of money out of our accounts." Once again the room was silent.

An older man in the back stood up. "We already know that Mr. Ferrell. What are we supposed to do now?"

"We have to find some money and quickly. I want you all to go over all of your existing accounts and look for any available funds that we can use to clear up this mess. I will do the same. I want you all back here in one hour. Do you hear me, one hour?"

Once in his own office, Garrett poured himself a glass of brandy and sat down at his computer. *So, whoever you are, you think you're real smart. We'll see about that.* As each account came up it showed either a zero balance or that all the money had been transferred back to the companies that had provided the illegal funds. Garrett pushed his chair away from his desk. He was no longer anonymous. Once the press got hold of the identities of the companies he was dealing with, they could all be traced by the FBI. Garrett began to pale. He was a dead man. They would find him.

Hobart lightly knocked on Garrett's door and then opened it without waiting for an answer. "Mr. Ferrell, it's no use. No one can find any viable accounts."

"Get out! Tell everyone to leave!" The brandy glass crashed against the door and then there was silence.

Garrett picked up the telephone. "Elliott, I need you."

He was in trouble. Jakuta had tried to push over a biloba tree with his trunk. He wanted to reach the leaves that were still on the higher branches. He had pushed several times with all his weight against the tree. When the trunk of the biloba finally cracked in two, a large branch came crashing down across Jakuta's leg. The branch dissected the tree and became wedged deep in the ground. Jakuta's leg was trapped inside the vice of wood. Pulling with all his strength he could not free himself. He was unsteady on three legs and feared falling over. Jakuta would be too vunerable if that happened. He began to make a low guttural sound deep in his throat. A sound so low it seemed inaudible. A few hundred yards away a group of females were grazing in an open field. Yemeni lifted her head and unfurled her ears. Signaling to the others they followed her toward the sound. It took them only a few minutes to pull the branch away from the tree and free Jakuta's leg. It was their duty—to protect each other.

Chapter Thirty-Three

"What the hell did you do?" Michael screamed into the phone. "We were supposed to move slow on this to keep it from drawing so much attention. Now it's all over the papers and television."

"I did exactly as you told me to," Taylor replied. "When I left Carol everything was fine. We had made just the necessary transactions. I've been trying to reach her all morning. There isn't any answer. I'm on my way over there right now. I'll call you back as soon as I find out something." He hurriedly hung up the phone and grabbed his jacket off the back of the chair.

Michael stared at the headlines in the paper again.

FERRELL ENTERPRISES COLLAPSES.

The stock market took a nosedive today as one of its biggest investors, Ferrell Enterprises created a financial avalanche. The Ferrell group has released more than fifty million dollars into the market. According to a spokesperson for the company they feel that a computer error has caused all of their bank accounts to be closed and that there is no need for alarm. The situation would be rectified in a timely manner. The question on their stockholder's minds today is, where is the money? The FDIC will begin their investigation immediately to protect the government funds. Garrett Ferrell cannot be reached for comment.

Michael paced back and forth across the patio. Maybe he should go to New York. He wondered why Carol decided to blow the lid off of everything. The investigation into this sort of thing could take months. Knowing Garrett, he had probably already left the country and he would never find him. He was also sure Garrett had money stashed other places, too. It couldn't end this way. He had spent all this time making sure that Garrett would end up in jail and now it may never happen.

By late afternoon he had still not heard from Taylor or Carol and the airwaves were buzzing with the story. He couldn't wait any longer. After booking an early evening flight to New York, he packed a bag and drove to his office. Clearing up a few business matters, he gave instructions to his managers and left. He would rather sit in the airport than wait around any longer.

Waiting in the airport lounge, Michael finished his second straight-up scotch and watched the news of the Ferrell

Enterprises collapse on television. It was the same story crawling across the bottom of the screen over and over. Ordering another drink, he slid off the stool and headed to the restroom. When he returned to the lounge the breaking news sign was flashing on the screen. A newsman was sitting at a desk with a picture of Garrett Ferrell behind him. "The New York Police Department has just informed the media that the body of well-known entrepreneur, Garrett Ferrell, has been found in his home. Newsmen have surrounded Mr. Ferrell's home for the last twelve hours since the story broke that his company had been dissolved. Details of his death have not been released at this time."

Michael sat down on the stool, his arm hitting his drink and spilling it over. "Oh, sorry, I…" The bartender put his hand up indicating no problem. Within a few minutes a new drink sat in front of Michael. He stared at the screen in disbelief. *Garrett Ferrell was dead. He was actually dead. Did the son of a bitch kill himself or did one of his illegal clients get to him already? So if the company was gone and he was dead, it was over. Why didn't he feel satisfied? He should be jumping up and down, but that still wouldn't bring his father back. He still missed him so much.* A sob caught in his throat and he bolted from the lounge spilling another drink on the bar.

Michael ran through the terminal and out to the parking lot. He heard the last call for his flight as he was driving away. It would be stupid for him to go to New York. There was no one there he knew that could tell him what happened. He would have to wait to hear from Taylor. He dialed his cell phone and waited. "Hi, this is Shay Young. Please leave a message and I will call you back." He waited for the beep.

"Shay, I need you. If you are in town please come to my house."

He was asleep on the sofa in the den when she arrived. He heard the key in the lock and the door open. She silently crossed the room and knelt down next to him. "Michael, I'm here," she whispered.

Michael wrapped his arms around her and let out a choking sob. She rubbed her hand across his face and lay down next to him telling him over and over how sorry she was for what happened between her and Elliott.

Michael finally put his fingers on her lips and said they would figure it all out in the morning. His hands traveled over her body. She responded with a long, deep kiss. They made love on the floor and fell asleep in each other's arms. It was a bittersweet reunion.

Shay sat the pitcher of orange juice and two glasses on the patio table. She pulled her robe around her and sat down across from Michael. "Did you sleep well?' she asked.

He smiled. "I don't remember." He reached across the table and took her hand. "I have something I want to tell you. It's a long story and pretty incredible, but I want you to know what is going on in my life. We better make a big pot of coffee."

She rested her chin on her hands. "Okay, I'm listening."

He told her everything. He started at the very beginning when his father first got promoted to the nineteenth floor. He told her about his relationship with his father and how he felt after he was told his father killed himself and then found out that he had been murdered. There was the whole mess with Carol and the papers and the twenty-seven million dollars. Shay listened without interrupting him, occasionally shaking her head in disbelief.

"And so when I heard that Garrett's company had fallen apart and he was dead, I realized that I really felt nothing. But, now I don't know where Taylor or Carol are and I haven't even a vague idea how to deal with Elliott. All I know is that I want to go to Rome and get my mother. I miss her and I want her back with me."

"Were you really going to kill him, Michael?"

"I don't know. At first that was all I could think about, but as time went on I changed my mind. After I met you it sort of took a back seat for a while. I hired Taylor and let him handle everything. He took on the task with vengeance as if it was his own personal vendetta. I didn't expect it would happen this quickly."

"This is all so unbelievable. So Garrett killed a lot of people and he may have even killed you. I can't imagine how you have handled this all this time. What about the twenty-seven million? What are you going to do with it?"

"At some point I thought I didn't deserve it. It was money Garrett made illegally, but he owed me that. My father's life was worth a lot more. I think I'm going to become the biggest commercial mortgage company in the state of California. I have about nineteen million left in the account and it can take me a long way."

"Sounds like you're trying to build more wealth than Garrett. Don't do that to yourself, Michael. When you start loving money more than the people around you, your life will turn into a nightmare just like Garrett's. Trust me, I've been there. When I started making a lot of money I thought I was on top of the world and all it brought me was a lot of unhappiness. Money isn't everything."

"Tell that to someone who doesn't have a lot of money. I'm not at all like Garrett. Don't even use my name in the same sentence with his." He was angry and she knew it.

"I'm sorry," she said, softly.

He began to pace back and forth across the patio. "I wish Taylor would call. I can't do anything until I hear from him. I still don't even know how Garrett died." He had barely finished the sentence when the phone rang.

"Just listen very carefully to what I have to say, Michael and then I'll answer all your questions. I want you to stay out of New York for at least a month. The federal agents are tearing the Ferrell building apart. They have confiscated every file, and even the paper in the wastebaskets. They're questioning everyone from the top on down to the janitors. A lot of the men from the nineteenth floor have disappeared and are on a hot list. I haven't seen any evidence of your name showing up, but of course Carol's name is on the list. The good news is that I feel you're in the clear, so let's keep it that way. Now, do you have any questions?"

"You're damn right I do. Do they know how Garrett died and what about Elliott? Has anyone seen him? And…where in the hell are you?"

"Garrett was shot point blank in the forehead. His body was propped up against the wall in his den between two elephant heads. It looks like a professional job. The police don't even have a fingerprint to go by. It took me a few thousand dollars in bribes, but I found out that Elliot took his father's airplane and his destination was listed as Mozambique. I think you know the place I'm talking about. I'm sure that Carol has left the country by now. I guess this pretty much wraps up everything I can do for you, Michael. This will probably be our last contact. I'm going to take a few months off. My mind is fried and I need some R and R."

"Thanks for everything, Taylor. Do I owe you any more money?"

"No, I'm fine. Have a good life, Michael. Don't dig yourself into any holes."

After Taylor hung up the telephone, he poured himself a drink and stepped out onto the small balcony over looking the town. He took a deep breath of the fresh air, admiring the snow-covered peaks in his view. He loved St. Moritz. Maybe he would stay here forever.

"Did you call Michael?"

"Yes."

"Did he ask about me?'

"He sure did, Peggy. I told him I didn't know where you were."

She continued to dry her hair with the bath towel as she stepped outside. "After we retrieve the money where do you want to go?" she asked.

"I like it here. Let's stay put for a while. How much do we have?"

"More than we can spend." She began to laugh and dance around the room, waving the towel in the air.

"Yep, I should say, we'll be okay." Taylor said, grinning. He took her into his arms and ran his hands through her wet hair. He could get used to her. She was better in bed than he expected and brilliant when it came to finances. With Garrett dead and a ton of money at his disposal, he could get used to almost anything right now.

Jakuta was alone once again wandering the Savannah. The herd of females and the following group of young males were miles in front of him. He had stopped at the watering hole and submerged himself in the cool water that quickly turned into a pool of mud. After drinking enough water to hold him for a few days and his back caked with mud to shield him from the blistering sun, he continued on his journey.

Chapter Thirty-Four

When the story about Garrett and his company began to wane and the articles about him were moved to the back section of the paper, Michael decided it would be safe to travel out of the country. He wanted to go to Rome and see his mother. The words that his father had said to him shortly before his death echoed in his head. *Remember, Son, if anything happens to me you take care of your mother and make sure she has a good life.* After visiting with his mother he was going to Africa to have his confrontation with Elliott. He had to find out why Elliott went off to Africa without telling him. Michael thought he would at least stay in the states long enough to see his father buried. Something had caused him to leave without even calling Michael. It was time for Elliott to know the whole story.

His relationship with Shay had grown, but he still felt uncomfortable leaving her. She had three or four assignments that she had put off while she was separated from Michael. It would be a good time for her to catch up on her work. Shay was uneasy about Michael going to see Elliott but she knew until he talked to him face to face he would never be able to put all of the mess from the last year behind him.

"Now, don't forget to call me as soon as you get to Rome. I'll be waiting for your call." She kissed him good-bye and watched until he had turned the corner in the airport and was out of sight. "Please, Michael, come back to me. I love you," she whispered to herself.

Arriving in Rome, Michael went directly to the convent without even checking into a hotel. He put his bags in a corner of the entryway and rang the bell on the desk. It was Sister Angelina who greeted him. She gave him a quick hug and escorted him out to the back veranda. His mother sat with an open book on her lap, and her glasses in her hand. She was asleep. Sister Angelina giggled. "We all say we are coming out here to read the bible, but we slip in a short nap." Her voice woke Rosa.

"My goodness, Michael. I thought I was dreaming."

Michael gave his mother a warm greeting and sat down next to her. "How are you, Mom? Is everything okay?"

"I'm fine, Michael."

He had no idea how or when he would tell her, but suddenly he felt as if he didn't tell her right away he may never be able to say the words.

"Mom, I've come here to tell you something. It's something about Dad that I think you should know. I was going to wait a couple of days to tell you, but I've decided to let you know so we will have time to talk about it." Michael began the story that he had told several times before. The story that resounded in his head like a tape recording of something he would like to erase forever. "…And so you see, Dad didn't commit suicide. He was murdered."

Rosa covered her face with her hands and rocked back and forth. "Oh, Frank. My poor Frank. If only he would have shared what was going on with me. Maybe I could have helped him. Why would he ever think we needed so much money?"

Michael handed her his handkerchief. "I don't think anyone could have helped him. Once Garrett got his claws into him, there was no turning back. Garrett Ferrell was an evil, sadistic man and he would have found some way to hurt us all. Dad knew that and he was trying to protect us." He put his arm around his mother. "Don't cry anymore, Mom. You know the truth so you don't have to suffer thinking that Dad was depressed enough to kill himself. Garrett is dead and you and I are safe now. I want to take you back to the states and you can come live with me. I promised Dad I would take care of you."

Rosa touched his face. "Now that I know the truth I have to take time to deal with it. Besides, my life is here and I feel safe. What would I do in California? You would be away at work and I would be alone. Besides you have your own life to live and I don't want you to change it for me. I have the Sisters around me all the time. When I'm sad they comfort me and when I'm happy, we laugh together. I have my own little garden to tend and a big kitchen to cook in. We go on bus trips to the small villages and markets and we pray. I know you made him a promise, but you've fulfilled his wish when you brought me here. As long as you promise to come visit me at least twice a year I'll be happy."

Even with trying to convince her that she wouldn't be in his way and that she would make new friends, he knew she wasn't going to change her mind. There wasn't any reason to keep asking her if she was sure about her decision to stay at the convent. He knew she was.

The next few days with his mother convinced him even more that her decision to stay in Rome was the right one. She spoke with the Sisters in Italian and they smiled at him. He had no idea what they were saying but he was sure it was something that would embarrass him. They knew his mother well, maybe even better than he did and he was leaving her in their care. She asked him questions about some of things he had told her and he tried his best to answer them without upsetting her.

Leaning against the taxi, Michael held his mother's small hand. "I have someone in my life that I care about. It may be serious and the next time I come to see you I am going to bring her along if that's okay with you."

"I will be waiting. I want to meet the person that is good enough for my son and may someday make me a grandmother." She put her arms around him and whispered, "I love you," in his ear. She looked into his eyes and smiled. "You are a good boy, Michael. Your father would be very proud of you."

As he drove away he somehow felt that he had not only lost his father, but now his mother was lost from his too. He wanted her in his life, not thousands of miles away.

The elephants gathered under the acacia trees in a tight group. A storm was coming. Not cooling rain, but the ominous red dust that would swirl around them for hours or even days. The thick powder would cover them completely leaving them unable to see what was ahead of them.

Chapter Thirty-Five

After seventeen hours of travel, Michael's small commuter plane landed at the airport in Malawi. Another four hours lay ahead of him as he made arrangements with a driver to transport him to the EMO Safari Club. He scrunched down in the seat of the SUV and pulled his hat over his head. He tried to sleep as the vehicle bounced along the bone-jarring, corrugated ruts. When he reached his destination, Michael crawled out of the car and put his hands on his aching back. He had no idea what he was going to say to Elliott. Thoughts had been running through his head since he left New York, yet nothing seemed to fall into place.

Checking in at the desk, Michael inquired about Elliott. "Mr. Ferrell is staying in one of the bungalows. I'll call and see if he is in," the concierge said. "I have not seen him all day."

"No, that's okay. Just tell me where it is and I'll walk down there. Please have someone take my bags to my room." He remembered this place quite well. This is where he experienced the first wrath of Garrett Ferrell. Now it was time to face his son. This meeting may even be worse.

A drizzle of rain trickled down his back as Michael walked along the path leading to the maze of wooden bungalows scattered among the elegant grounds. When he reached number three, a shaft of light filtered through the bamboo shade that covered the window. Taking a deep breath, Michael knocked on the door. He knocked several times with no answer. He was weary from his trip. One more day couldn't make that much difference. Back in his room he was lulled to sleep in the African world of shadows and strange sounds.

With the smell of smoke close to his face, Michael sat straight up in bed. Sitting next to him, a cigarette dangling from his mouth, was a resemblance of someone he once knew. Dressed only in a pair of soiled field shorts and sporting a growth of bushy, red beard, Michael barely recognized Elliott in his disheveled condition.

"What are you doing here?" were the first words Michael was greeted with.

"I came to find you," Michael said as he got out of bed and put on his pants. He watched as Elliott paced back and forth across the small space, taking deep drags off the cigarette. He seemed disjointed, his eyes darting from side to side. He put the butt on the floor and stepped on it. "Did you come here to gloat? Now that my father is dead and I'm penniless I bet you feel really good," Elliott said in a sarcastic tone. "I hear some-one coming? Did you bring someone with you? Are you being followed?'

"What's wrong with you? Are you on something?" Michael asked.

Elliott let out a loud laugh. "What's wrong with me! Because of you the company that was supposed to be mine is gone. The Feds confiscated everything my family owned—both of our houses, the yacht, all our cars and anything else they could get their hands on. The press has followed my every move until I was able to slip out on them. And my plane almost went down on the way here. I got nothing, zero, nada. I'm glad you decided to pay me this visit. We can settle the score right now. Oh, by the way, how is your little girlfriend?"

Michael closed his hands into fists. He was ready to punch Elliott in the face. He could sense that it would be useless to try and talk to Elliott in the condition he was in, but he was going to try. "I want to talk about what has gone on in the past year. We need to get some things straight."

Elliott let out a loud laugh. "What? That I can have Shay anytime I want."

Michael rushed toward Elliott and swung at his face, catching him on the chin. The blow sent Elliot crashing into the side of the dresser and tumbling to the floor. He struggled to his feet, wiping the blood from his lip. "This isn't over yet, Michael. In fact, it has just begun." He staggered toward the door. Elliott turned and pointed his finger at Michael. "I'll be back this afternoon. Don't go anywhere."

It was all a little worse than Michael had expected. Elliott seemed completely irrational and it was going to be hard to deal with him. He rubbed his fist. Michael had hit Elliott only once before. It was in a bar, they were both drunk and arguing over a point on the dartboard. When he hit him, they both fell down and laid on the floor laughing. No one was laughing now. Maybe he should just give him the money and let it be over with, but that would mean Elliott had won. His father's death would have been for nothing. He couldn't let that happen.

By early afternoon the temperature soared to almost 100 degrees and the hot air was stifling. Michael dressed in shorts and a cotton shirt and went downstairs to the lounge. He ordered a tall scotch and water and sat down at a table near the window. Half way through his drink Elliott appeared at the door and loudly called out his name. The few people in the lounge stopped talking and looked over at him. Michael got up and went to the door. "Come on, let's go sit down and we can talk."

"No!" Elliott replied in a loud voice. "You come with me."

"Where are we going?" Michael asked. "It looks like it's getting ready to storm." Rather than cause a scene, Michael finished his drink and followed Elliott outside.

Pulling keys from his pocket Elliott pointed to the mud-covered jeep sitting in front of the compound entrance.

Elliott had just started the jeep and began backing up when two men came running down the path waving their hands in the air. One began yelling. "Stop! Stop the vehicle. You can't go into the bush without a guide."

Elliott continued to back up. The men jumped to the side of the road as Elliott passed by them.

"Dammit, you almost ran over them, Elliott. You'd better go back."

"Screw them. I don't need a guide. I know exactly where I'm going."

A few hundred feet down the rutted path he veered off the road and headed up a steep slope. "Hold on to your hat. This is a hell of a ride," Elliott yelled over the roar of the motor. Clouds of dusts jumped out at them as small herds of animals ran in front of the jeep. Michael ducked his head to miss the branches that were smacking into the metal. Elliott seemed to be oblivious to the jarring motion and pushed forward even when the jeep ran into large rocks that almost turned it on its side. When the ridge finally seemed to drop away and meet the sky he came to a stop in a small clearing.

Pulling out two high-powered rifles and a pair of binoculars, Elliott motioned to Michael to follow him. He began to crouch down and creep toward the rim. "Get down," he whispered. Michael fell to his knees and crawled up next to Elliott. "Look down there, over to your right." He handed the binoculars to Michael. Spanning the valley below him, Michael's eyes finally rested on a herd of elephants barely visible behind the thick brush. "Am I supposed to be looking at elephants?" he asked.

"You bet you are. Guess who is hanging around the herd? Good old white ear. The big bull my father tried to kill for over twenty years. And now he's mine. Wouldn't that piss my father off big time? I've been watching him all week."

"Look, Elliott, if you want to kill an elephant that's your business. I didn't come all the way to Africa to join you in a hunt. We need to talk. Can we go back to the club?"

"Sure, after I bag him. He'll be circling around the herd for a while and then he'll head up this way to feed. Here," he said, tossing one of the guns to Michael.

"Dammit, Elliott, what's the matter with you? You know I'm not a hunter. I don't like killing animals."

Elliott pulled a flask out of his pocket and took a long drink. "How about people? Weren't you planning on killing my father? I know everything. I know all about your dad and the business and the men my old man killed. He told me everything."

"I wanted to kill him at first. I was so angry that's all I could think about. But I couldn't do it."

"But all the time you were pretending to be my friend you were slowly destroying my life."

"If my plan would have played itself out I would have made sure you were taken care of, Elliott."

"Oh, that's real big of you, Michael. Just how were you going to do that?"

"I was going to split the money with you. With fourteen million dollars you would have been okay. How did you find out about everything? When did your father tell you?" Michael asked.

"Right before I killed him." Making his fingers into the shape of a gun he pointed at Michael. "Bang! One shot, right between the eyes. I killed him and now I'm going to kill his elephant."

Michael's eyes widened. He was stunned. "What did you say?"

"I said…I killed him. I killed my father." Elliott let out a laugh. "Damn, don't look so surprised. Somebody had to do it." He took another long drink.

"But I thought he was killed by someone that he screwed out of money. You're lying."

"Afraid not, Pal. He called me and I rescued him from his office the day his business collapsed. He was shaking all over. He told me everything in the car on the way to the house. He spilled his guts about the illegal dealings, the dummy companies and the people he did away with. He even told me at one time he had plotted to kill my mother."

"Did he say anything at all about my father?" Michael asked.

"He said your old man was a good guy, but he got in the way. Even our friendship couldn't keep him alive."

A streak of lightning zigzagged across the dark-blue sky, followed by a low rumble of thunder.

"Anyway I got him out of his office and back to the house through the side entrance. When we got inside his whole demeanor changed. He started acting real crazy. He said we had to stick together. Then the next minute he was telling me that he needed to leave the country and the only way we could do that was to get the money your father took from the company. He said it was twenty-seven million. Is that right, Michael?" Elliott continued on without waiting for an answer. "He started telling me how clever you were and that he admired you for that. He said I should have been more like you and that I was worthless and would never make anything of myself. I couldn't believe how crazy he was acting. He took a gun out of his desk drawer and handed it to me. He told me I should just go ahead and kill myself if I didn't plan on helping him get the money, because we were both dead men anyway. All I could see in front of me was a broken, useless person who I have hated all my life. He was of no use to me anymore. I picked up the gun and called his name. He turned and I fired. Just one shot blew him back against the wall. I left the house by the side gate, climbed over the fence and went straight to the airport. Tell me how you did it, Michael? How could someone like you destroy a company like Ferrell?"

"I had help. I told you it wasn't supposed to play out this way, but sooner or later I planned on getting even with your father. And now I find out that you did it for me. Too bad you waited so long."

The wind began to blow small pockets of dust across the ridge as the smell of rain permeated the air. "We need to go back to the camp. It's going to storm any minute," Michael said, standing up.

"Sit down! We're not going anywhere. I said…sit down." Elliott's rifle was now pointing in Michael's direction. "We've got some business to settle, pal. Now for the twenty-seven million dollar question? Where is the money?"

"So that's what this is all about, money. I should have known that. You've always been all about money."

"Really. What else did I have? Do you think it was fun watching you and your little family? All of your dinners together and your game night, when my parents couldn't even make it home for Christmas. Even in college you always were the shining star. Do you really know how jealous I was of you? Yeah, sure, we had fun. You were always my greatest challenge and if you remember, you were my only friend. Then you come out smelling like a rose after your father dies—new business and my girlfriend."

Michael wiped the rain from his face. "My father didn't die. He was murdered. I would have given anything to keep him alive. So I guess that made you happy…me not having a father. When I get back to the states I'll send the money anywhere you want. I don't want any of it. I just want this all to be over. I'm going back to camp. Are you coming?" He started to walk toward the jeep while Elliott still sat with his rifle on his lap.

"I want Shay, too and then we'll be even," Elliott said, loudly. "She was mine first and I want her back."

Michael whirled around. "You son of a bitch! There is no way we will ever be even, Elliott. You stay away from Shay!"

Bolts of lightning were now pelting the grasslands below the ridge and the ominous green sky turning daylight to night. Neither of them were aware that all of the elephants, except for one had moved out of the open plain. The big bull had stayed behind as the others sought cover. His ears flared as he rocked back and forth.

Jakuta had heard their voices. One in particular was familiar to him. A vision of his mother lying dead came into his head. Two men had stood over her. One of them was here now. His curiosity may well get him killed. Staying below the ridge the elephant made his way up the far side of the slope. Hidden by the cover of darkness and the blinding rain, Jakuta was within one hundred feet of the two men on the ridge and still unnoticed by them.

Michael opened the door of the jeep just as the elephant broke loose from his cover and closed in on them. "Elliott, get up, get up…the elephant," Michael shouted.

Elliott scrambled to his feet, grabbing for his rifle, but it was too late. Jakuta was upon him. With one fell swoop he picked Elliott up in his trunk and hurled him in the air. Elliott screamed as his body crumpled to the ground. Scrambling for his rifle, Elliott aimed at the elephant and squeezed the trigger. The bullet hit the lower tip of the Jakuta's ear. Lowering his head, Jakuta charged again, pinning Elliott to the tree with his left tusk. Pulling back, blood dripped off the tip of the ivory spear.

Michael was astounded. His gun still lay on the ground where he had left it. It was now between him and the elephant.

As the rain poured off his back, Jakuta turned. He looked at Michael, who was now standing behind the door of the jeep, too petrified to move.

Jakuta stared at him. He had no recollection of this man. He was not a hunter. He had no quarrel with him. Jakuta gave one last warning. He shook his head back and forth and pounded the ground with his enormous feet before moving off down the hill.

Michael ran to Elliott. He knelt down and gathered Elliott into his arms. The pool of blood oozing from the gaping hole in his side turned to a muddy red as it seeped onto the ground. Elliott's eyes were closed.

Michael knew it was no use to try and move him. He was almost lifeless. Elliott slowly opened his eyes. "Did you kill him?" he whispered.

"Yes, I got him," Michael lied.

"Good, then we're even, friend." His head slumped forward.

Michael cradled Elliott's lifeless body. "I'm sorry. I didn't expect it to end this way. I just wanted your father to pay for his sins. Not you. I'm sorry, Elliott."

In the morning, Michael stood at the desk at the Safari Club. "Elliott's mother has arranged for his body to be shipped back to the states in a few days," he said to the concierge. "I'm leaving today."

"I'm so sorry for what has happened to your friend," the man said. "This has never happened in all my years working here. It's just that Elliott was like his father. They did not like to follow the rules. It was an unfortunate accident."

"Yes, I know. They were both rebels and it cost them their lives."

"And you, Mr. Charpelli, what are your plans?"

"I'm going back to Los Angeles and try to start my life over."

"Good luck to you."

Less than twenty-four hours later the game warden dispatched a troop of park rangers into the Savannah to find the rogue elephant that killed Elliott. They tracked him across the open plain and into the thicket. Surrounded and nowhere to go Jakuta burst out of the brush giving one last resounding bellow. It took thirteen shots to bring him down.

His tusks were removed and sold to help support the game preserve. His body was left as food for the predators that roamed the Savannah. Young bulls would pass by the piles of bones that were all that was left of the mighty elephant. Touching the remains they were now aware that a new bull would soon take his place.

Five Years Later

A young bull elephant stood in the lush grass of the Savannah. He enjoyed the richness of the summer season. Just a few hundred feet away a herd of female elephants grazed in the afternoon sun. He would have his pick of the herd. No one would challenge him. He was in the prime of his life. He was the son of Jakuta.

Michael Charpelli picked up the telephone in his luxurious office. "I'm sorry, Shay. I have a lot to do before I can make it home tonight."

"But, Michael, you haven't seen our children all week. They miss you."

"I promise, tomorrow night I'll be home early. Kiss them goodnight for me. I have to go I have someone in my office."

Shelia Glass smoothed the skirt of her Chanel suit. "So what do you think, Michael? Are you interested in this property?"

"I could be, if the price is right and I can get all the inspection permits it will take before we can start work on it."

"You know there are ways to get around them, Michael. It may cost a few dollars, but think of all the money you will make on property if you can tear it down right away. We need to move quickly before the present owners are able to raise the money and save foreclosure."

"Is it anybody we know?" he asked.

"No, just a few small mom and pop businesses. Nothing of any significance to us."

"Good, let's do it. Now, I need a drink. Are you in a hurry to get home?"

And so the Circle of Prey begins again.

The End

For more information on Marlene Mitchell or any of her awesome novels, go to:

www.bearheadpublishing.com/marlene.html

LaVergne, TN USA
15 February 2010
173126LV00003BA/14/P

9 780979 915383